YOURS I HAVE

A PURE DECADENCE NOVEL

KELLY COLLINS

BOOK NOOK PRESS

Copyright © 2020 by Kelly Collins

No part of this publication may be reproduced, distributed, or transmitted in any form or by any means, including photocopying, recording, or other electronic or mechanical methods, without the prior written permission of the publisher, except as permitted by U.S. copyright law. For permission requests, contact kelly@authorkellycollins.com.

The story, all names, characters, and incidents portrayed in this production are fictitious. No identification with actual persons (living or deceased), places, buildings, and products is intended or should be inferred. All products or brand names are trademarks of their respective owners.

CHAPTER ONE

"Kat, it's just dinner. No one's asking you to get naked. He needs a companion for the fundraiser tonight," Emma says as she looks at me with puppy dog eyes. "I've gone to several of these events with him, and he's always been a gentleman. The man keeps his professional life separated from his personal life. Hell, I'm not even sure he has a personal life."

Falling to her knees in front of me, Em closes her eyes as if in prayer. "Damon is the type of male perfection you only find on the pages of magazines. He reminds me of Alexander Skarsgård, although Alexander's eyes are a different color blue, and his hair is blond. The client is a tall, dark-haired, blue-eyed Viking. He's harmless, Kat. In fact, I think he may be gay because he's never dated anyone that I'm aware of."

Em gets up from her knees and stands in front of me with her hands steepled in prayer. "Please, Kat," she begs. "I need you to do this for me. I screwed up and overbooked tonight. I can't be with two men at the same time. Besides, we'll be at the same event, so if you feel uncomfortable, I'll be close by."

"Won't your client care?" I ask.

"I asked Damon if he would mind the switch, and he assured me it wouldn't be a problem." She dropped to her knees again. "Please help me out. Pleeease."

I look into her eyes as they silently plead her case. I know she would bail me out if I needed her, but this is extreme.

"I don't think I can do it, Em. I mean ... what am I supposed to do? I have no training as an escort." I watch her face fall into a frown. "That's your thing, not mine." I shake my head. "I've always known someday you would get yourself into trouble, but I never thought it would involve me."

With a roll of her eyes, she hops to her feet. "You act as if I'm asking you to prostitute yourself." Her lips purse and then relax. "I run a legitimate escort service. I'm not a hooker. I don't sleep with my clients." She sighs, then continues. "Well, that's not altogether true. I slept with Mark, but it was because I wanted to, not because he paid me."

The thought of accompanying a complete stranger to a formal event terrifies me. My stomach feels like I've just crested the highest peak of a roller coaster, and I'm descending at record speed.

"Em, I want to help you, but I don't have the foggiest idea how to behave in this situation."

She stops and closes her eyes. I can only imagine how fast she is flipping through the Rolodex in her brain to come up with an example. Her head tilts toward the ceiling while her lips scrunch up—this is her thinking face. Within seconds, she lights up, and I know I'm in trouble. Emma has a way of coming up with the perfect scenario that will work in her best interest.

"Remember when we went with your parents to the ballet? We dressed up—you in the pink dress and me in the light-blue one." She stares at me as if waiting for a light bulb to illuminate over my head. "Do you remember how we had to socialize with all your dad's clients before and after the event?"

"Yes, and I also remember it was the most boring night of my life."

Smiling, she says, "This will be just like that night, except you might like some of people you meet, and you'll make three hundred dollars. All you have to do is look pretty and smile." She fluffs her hair and shows off her pearly whites. "You'll also get to wear one of my fabulous formal gowns. Just say yes!"

Emma is back on her knees in front of me, pleading. I have a soft spot for her, so despite my fear, I agree to help. "Okay! Just stand up and stop begging. I'll help you out this one time, but I want to wear your red gown, and you have to do my hair. If the guy is a total creep, I'm leaving, and you're paying for the taxi."

Jumping up and down, Emma dances around me. "Oh, my God, I knew you wouldn't let me down. He'll be here to pick you up at seven o'clock. It's a hospital fundraiser, and Damon is a benefactor. There will be live music and dancing afterward." Emma wraps me in a big hug. "Kat, you're the best friend ever."

"You'll owe me big time for this one." I give her my most intimidating look, which isn't scary at all. I need to work on that. "Let me jump in the shower, and when I'm done, you're up because I have just over an hour to get ready." I walk toward the bathroom, removing my clothes along the way.

"I'll have you ready in thirty minutes because that's how good I am."

"Whatever." Looking down at my toes, I smile. "You're lucky I had a mani-pedi yesterday. Otherwise, I'd need an outfit that goes with boots and gloves." Stopping, I turn to ask her a question that has bounced in my brain for a few minutes. "Why do I get this guy instead of the one you're escorting tonight?"

Taking a deep breath, she answers. "I know Damon will be a gentleman. The other guy is an unknown." She shrugs her shoulders. "I've never accompanied him. I imagine he'll be nice, but since I don't know him personally, I don't feel comfortable having you escort him." She waves her hand at me dismissively. "Go take your shower so I can get you all dolled up."

I shampoo my hair, shave my legs, and ready myself for "work." My body wash smells of coconut and mango and makes me think of somewhere exotic like Fiji. Wouldn't it be nice to escape somewhere else for the night?

A tropical island sounds good right now. I'd love to be anywhere but here. Covering for Emma petrifies me because I'm way out of my league. I mean, I don't even date regularly. Who has time between work and school?

My life is barely in balance as it is, and tonight the scales will tilt toward pure chaos.

CHAPTER TWO

"Kat, you look stunning—truly beautiful." Em stands back to look at me. She walks around me, smoothing my hair, and wiping a smudge of mascara from under my eye. "Everything is just perfect," she declares.

"You really know how to turn a duckling into a swan."

I saw myself in the full-length mirror before I made my debut into the living room. The results were nothing less than miraculous.

Cut on the bias, the red dress clings nicely to my figure. Emma pulled my hair up into a French knot she secured with a pretty bejeweled hair comb.

My makeup looks elegant and soft. The lipstick is too bright for my taste, but since I'm wearing a red dress, I can see where she was going with it.

"Who are you going with, Em?"

"I'll be accompanying Anthony Haywood."

"Anthony Haywood, the restaurateur?" My mouth drops open in shock. "*That* Anthony Haywood?"

Anthony Haywood owns a chain of upscale restaurants all over the world. He is a mega-millionaire, reported to be one of the world's most eligible bachelors. I recently read a fascinating article about him. A real rags-to-riches story.

"Wow! That's some date you have."

"It's not a date, Kat. It's a job. But yes, I think he'll be an interesting companion. You, my dear, will accompany Damon Noble."

My jaw drops at the mention of his full name. He's the owner of a chain of exclusive nightclubs called Zenith.

"Close your mouth. I told you I have an elite client list who just want an educated, attractive woman on their arms. Relationships and romance don't interest these men because they're too busy conquering the world to have time to date. You know how this works."

"I know how it works for you, but I've never considered your line of work for myself."

"I'm just a pretty face for hire. And tonight, so are you."

Em darts out of the room to ready herself; she's used to this lifestyle and has her routine down pat. She emerges wearing a navy-blue gown cut obscenely low in the front. I'm not sure how her breasts are staying inside the dress, but I'm so glad I didn't ask to wear blue.

I don't have the courage or cleavage to pull that dress off. Her hair hangs in waves around her shoulders. She reminds me of Jessica Rabbit with her red hair and curves in all the right places.

The sound of the doorbell interrupts my thoughts, and my heart beats out a frantic tattoo as Em glides slowly to the door.

"That should be Damon. I didn't want there to be a bottleneck at the door, so my client will arrive at seven-fifteen. Let me look at you one more time." She gives me a once-over before she smiles and tells me I'm flawless.

There's a cyclone turning in my stomach that threatens to rise up and choke me. I move to the side and let Emma care for her client.

"Hi, Damon. Come on in. Katarina is all set to go." She leans in and kisses his cheek. "Thank you for your flexibility. I can't figure out how this happened." Emma steps aside so he can enter the foyer.

"It's not a problem. You know how much I hate these things. Thankfully, I only have to attend a few of them a year." His eyes scan the room and lock on mine. "It doesn't matter who comes with me as long as someone does. Attending these alone is the worst." He talks to Em, but his eyes stay on me. He looks me over, and after a minute of silence, he smiles. Walking over, he offers his arm. "Katarina Cross, I presume?"

Wow. She wasn't kidding. He's a gorgeous man. Tall with espresso colored hair and blue eyes, he's a real treat to look at dressed in his tuxedo. Maybe this won't be so bad.

"Yes, but you can call me Kat if you'd like."

His smile tightens. "I'd prefer to call you Katarina, and you can call me Damon for the evening. Shall we go?" His voice is smooth and sophisticated. It slides over me like warm honey.

"See you soon," Emma calls out as Damon escorts me to the waiting limousine.

At the end of the sidewalk, a driver waits with the door open. Standing aside, he aids my entrance into the black stretch limo. I situate my dress, placing my small purse on my lap. The slit rides up my leg, leaving several inches of thigh exposed. No adjusting seems to pull it under control.

Seated across from me, Damon stares at my legs before his attention turns to my face. This man is definitely not gay. There is a gleam in his eyes, and his close inspection of me makes me squirm, causing the dress to ride up even farther.

His eyes drift back to my exposed leg. I grab my handbag and pull it to my center, like a shield, as if my three-inch-by-five-inch purse can protect me.

"You look nervous, Katarina. What can I do to make you more comfortable?" he asks. "Maybe a glass of wine will calm your nerves.

Would you like one?" He looks directly into my eyes, waiting for my response.

"Thank you. That would be lovely. Just a small glass, please. I haven't eaten much today, and I don't want the alcohol to go to my head."

He leans over me to reach for the decanter of red wine. The scent of him wafts under my nose as he fills the glass and places it into my shaking hands.

"Am I drinking by myself?" I ask.

He nods, sending a sweep of bangs across his forehead. "I never mix alcohol with business. People who drink too much make poor decisions." He swipes the hair back and continues to study me.

I respect his decision not to drink. I'd abstain myself if I weren't so nervous.

"We have a thirty-minute drive before we arrive at our destination. Tell me something about yourself. I'd like to get to know you."

"I'm not a professional escort," I say matter-of-factly. I don't know why I feel the need to say this, but somehow it makes me feel better about myself.

Chuckling, he says, "I know. Emma said you're her roommate. Tell me something I don't know."

"I'm a senior at UCLA, studying hospitality management, and also getting a minor in accounting."

His eyes widen in surprise. "I graduated from UCLA with a degree in business management. We already have something in common. The two degrees are similar, except yours is more specific."

"I'm certain I'll enjoy working in the field, but my focus is on graduating." I nervously pull at my dress to see if I can stop it from rising. If I don't, by the time we arrive at the venue, it's liable to be hiked up to my neck.

A knowing smile breaks from his lips. He seems to enjoy my discomfort. "I'm sure school keeps you busy, but what do you do for fun?" he asks.

"Fun?" I chuckle. "I don't know what that means." I take a sip of wine and continue. "I work full-time and go to school. There isn't much time for fun."

His fingers tap on the seat next to him, and I wonder if it's a nervous gesture or if he does it unconsciously.

"You know, they say all work and no play makes Katarina a tired girl."

I respond to his incorrect recitation. "I think the correct saying is 'All work and no play makes Kat a dull girl.'"

"Are you a dull girl? Maybe your job makes you more exciting. Where do you work?"

He doesn't care where I work, but I play along. In fact, I want to see how much of his attention I have. Is he genuinely interested in what I have to say, or is he going through the motions of being polite?

"I'm a stripper at Baby Dolls," I declare.

His eyes dart from my legs to my face. I imagine he's looking to see if there is any truth in my statement. His fingers immediately stop bouncing against the seat, and I laugh at his reaction. It pleases me to see he is paying attention.

"Somehow, I don't see you pole dancing at Baby Dolls." He leans forward and places his elbows on his knees. His new position divides the distance between us.

I continue to giggle and think maybe a glass of wine was too much.

"Oh, no, I'm much too uncoordinated to use the pole. I'm a cage dancer," I tease.

He grins and continues to toy with me. "I know, without a doubt, Baby Dolls has no cage dancers. I find it highly unlikely you work there. Since the mere rising of your gown makes you blush, I can't imagine you dancing naked." The tapping begins again, only this time with just his index finger on his chin.

"So, you're a patron?" I give him a pointed stare. "I guess you caught me in a fib." With a tilt of my head, I shrug. "I work at

Java Joes. If you want a great cup of coffee, then come see me. If you want a lap dance, you'll need to look elsewhere." My statement lets him know I have a sense of humor, but it also tells him I don't plan on offering him anything beyond platonic companionship.

"Darn. I was thinking Baby Dolls upped their game. If you worked there, I'd consider a visit. It's not my usual, but I'd stray off the beaten path to see you dance." His hand lowers, and he drums his fingers on the seat again.

"Flattery will get you nowhere, Mr. Noble." I lower my eyes and smile sweetly in his direction. It's the best imitation of coy I can muster.

At least he's fun and flirtatious, and I feel comfortable in his presence.

"I believe the saying is, 'Flattery will get you everywhere, Ms. Cross.'" His blue eyes smile at me as if he is waiting for me to counter.

"If flattery is all you've got, you need to step up your game."

His lips lift into a devilish grin that matches the twinkle in his eyes. "I'll take that as a challenge, Katarina."

I wasn't trying to challenge the man; I was just being playful. "Why do you insist on calling me Katarina?"

"It's your given name. If your parents wanted someone to call you Kat, they should have named you Kat." His eyes narrow. "Second, I looked it up before I picked you up tonight. It means pure, and after meeting you, I can see the purity in you. You are not a woman of the world, Katarina." He sits back and looks into my eyes. "Not a cat with sharp claws and a finicky personality. If you are a feline, you are a graceful and intelligent one with a nice touch of mischievousness and a good dose of innocence. It's such a beautiful name and perfect for you."

There's my heart again, beating wildly. How can his words throw me off balance so completely? How did he sum me up in less than fifty words? What does that say about me? I'm young, naïve, and maybe a little fun?

He's playful, sophisticated, and sexy. He's also off-limits. Deep in thought, I'm oblivious to our arrival until the car stops, and the door opens.

"Are you ready to go?" Damon stands outside of the car, extending his hand to help me exit. "Don't be nervous. It's just dinner." His smile is disarming. If you've never seen a Viking god smile, it's a sight to see.

I step out of the car as gracefully as one can in heels. He quickly places his hand in mine and confidently guides me up the stairs and into the building where an amalgamation of perfumes and colognes sits heavy in the air.

We stroll through the crowd together. Steering me from group to group, he introduces me to a broad range of people, from politicians to movie stars. Damon seems to know everyone. I would have thought I'd be starstruck by all the A-listers present, but I can't keep my mind off Damon Noble.

After an hour of smiling and mingling, the dinner bell rings, and we're herded into the dining room. He escorts me to the head table, where we will sit with the mayor and the board of directors from the hospital. As a major sponsor, they place Damon in a position of honor. He helps me into my chair before seating himself.

Sitting two tables away, I spot Emma. She winks at me and then turns her attention back to her escort, which reminds me that all my attention should be on Damon. As I turn to look at him, I find him gazing at me. It's as if he's trying to figure something out.

"What are you staring at?" I ask in a quiet voice, so I don't draw attention to our conversation.

"Just admiring how the light reflects off your hair. It has the most interesting effect. Turn your head in one direction, and it looks gold, but if you shift in another, the color turns to platinum. Tell me, if you were to let your hair down, where would it fall?" He reaches up and touches a strand of hair that's come loose, tucking it behind my ear.

His touch warms me.

"It falls midway down my back." Once again, I'm gifted with a broad smile.

A tap on my shoulder draws my attention away from Damon's hundred-watt grin. Looking up, I see Emma.

"Can I borrow Katarina for a minute?" We both look at him and wait for his response.

"Certainly, but don't be too long. It's almost time for dinner."

Emma and I walk to the bathroom, where we touch up our lipstick and powder our noses.

"How's it going?" Em asks.

"I think it's going well. He's charming, and, you were right, he has been an absolute gentleman. I don't think you did him justice when you were describing him. I mean, he is not only handsome but also engaging."

"Well, he isn't exactly *my* type in the looks department, and as far as engaging, I've never really seen that side of him. He's usually stoic." She kissed a Kleenex and tossed the red-stained tissue into the trash can. "I'm a little surprised at the way he looks at you. Normally, he's not attentive, but he's taken with you, Katarina." She giggles as she pronounces my name Kah-tah-ree-nah with the best foreign accent she can fake. She fails miserably, but it makes me laugh.

"He's just being nice," I reply.

"Damon isn't known for the after-dinner social scene. He'll probably stay a little while to be polite and then tuck you in a car and send you home."

"Oh, okay. Thanks for the heads-up. I have to study, so getting home at a decent hour will be great." I smile on the outside, but somewhere inside, I feel disappointed. I'm all dressed up and won't even get to dance, and there is no doubt in my mind that Damon would be an excellent dancer. "How is Anthony? Is he a nice man?"

"He's interesting." That's all she says as she guides me back to Damon.

He stands as I approach and helps me into my seat.

"I thought you had abandoned me or left with someone else," he says.

"Did I miss anything while I was gone?"

"Not unless you missed me." He quirks a brow.

I smirk at the silliness of his statement. "I guess I missed nothing, then."

He slaps his hand against his chest. "I'm wounded."

"Somehow, I doubt that, Mr. Noble."

Shortly after I take my seat, they serve dinner. The meal begins with a crisp salad and fresh bread.

Conversation continues to be lively as our table mates trade stories about their lives. I sit quietly and take it all in. Who would have thought I'd be dining with the mayor tonight? Who would have thought I'd be here with Damon Noble?

The woman to my right is on the board of directors at the hospital. Her name is Rose, and she's an oncologist. She engages me in a conversation about my education and says she is also an alumna of UCLA.

Looking at Damon, she asks, "Where did you find her? This one is a breath of fresh air."

"A mutual friend introduced us."

He stares at me with his glacier-blue eyes, and I find it hard to look away. There is something mesmerizing about the color of his irises. Some unseen force has fused my gaze to his, and the intensity of his look sets my heart fluttering.

"I hope you keep this one," the older woman says as if she has some say in Damon Noble's love life.

"I might keep her," he says with a hint of authority.

His hand covers mine, and he squeezes it gently. I'm uncertain what the squeeze means, but I assume it means to play along.

I lean over and give him a chaste kiss on the cheek that makes my lips tingle. "That was such a nice thing to say."

The moment is interrupted by our second course, which includes a beautifully prepared filet and a piece of salmon. The steak looks succulent and moist, and the salmon is cooked to perfection. I can tell everyone is enjoying their dinners by the silence at the table.

The lack of conversation gives me time to appreciate the room, which is gilded in gold and has large chandeliers hanging from the ceiling. An elegant floral arrangement decorates each table, and someone has placed name cards above each place setting. Mine says, "Guest."

"Did you enjoy your dinner, Katarina?" Damon uses the linen napkin to wipe his mouth and sets it on the table next to his near-empty plate.

"It was delicious. I especially liked the salmon. What about you?"

"The meal was nice, but I took pleasure in watching you eat. Did you know you chew everything at least twenty times?"

I giggled. "I don't exactly count to twenty, but I chew my food well, so I don't choke. I wouldn't want you to have to give me the Heimlich."

"In a room full of hospital staff, there would be someone more qualified to perform the task."

I look around at all the older guests. "You're probably right, but I'm sure they wouldn't be nearly as handsome or charming."

His eyes narrow. "Don't let me fool you," he whispers in a deep voice. "I'm a wolf in sheep's clothing."

"I'll consider myself warned." *What the hell?* "What do you think we'll have for dessert?" I ask.

He removes the program from under his plate and scans it until he finds the menu. "It looks like you will have pot de crème with raspberries and fresh whipped topping." Leaning back in his chair, he adjusts his cummerbund and smooths out the silky material with his long fingers.

"What about you? Don't you eat dessert?" I'm surprised someone would want to pass on a little pot of chocolate wonder.

"I don't indulge often."

"Well, that just seems criminal. No wine and no sweets? What do you indulge in?"

His eyes light up, and a wicked smile spreads across his face. "I can assure you I indulge. However, my tastes likely differ from yours. Enjoy your chocolate," he says.

"I'm intrigued." I want to explore the subject further.

"You're not ready." His salacious grin disappears as he sips his coffee, and I know we're not talking about cake.

As the master of ceremonies talks, Damon leans over and whispers in my ear. "Don't go anywhere because I'll be right back." He rises at the mention of his name and walks to the podium.

He takes control of the room and mesmerizes me. There's not a sound as everyone waits to hear what Damon Noble has to say.

"Ladies and gentlemen, thank you for coming out to dinner tonight. This fundraiser is near and dear to my heart. Over ten thousand children and young adults are diagnosed with some form of cancer each year. The five-year survival rate has increased from fifty-eight percent to nearly eighty percent since 1970. Your generous donations to research keep us moving forward in our search for a cure. I stand before you and ask you to give generously. Your dollar could be the one that saves a life."

As Damon steps down from the podium, the thunderous sound of applause is deafening. The master of ceremonies takes his place and waits for the crowd to settle down.

"If you enjoyed dinner tonight, thank Mr. Noble and his mother, Rose, for their commitment to the Los Angeles General Hospital and their continued support of cancer research. Please stay and enjoy the live music and dancing."

Rose is his mother? The information bounces back and forth in my head. Looking at her, I see the resemblance. She has similar blue eyes, although Damon's are brighter and bluer. Her hair looks almost silver, but it was probably a light blonde when she was younger. Feeling heat spread across my back, I turn and find him staring at me.

Can someone warm you with a look?

"Damon. Katarina." Rose says. "I'll leave you to enjoy the music. It's been my pleasure to meet you, young lady." Looking straight into Damon's eyes, his mother says, "I'd like to see her again."

He leans forward and kisses her cheek. "Good night, Mother. I'll talk to you soon."

After Rose leaves, I ask, "Why didn't you tell me she was your mother?" It seems odd he didn't introduce her as such.

"It didn't seem important." He shrugs my question off with a tip of his shoulder.

"I like her. She's nice."

"She has her moments." He stands and pulls me next to him. "Would you like to dance?"

Shocked by his invitation, I'm left speechless and confused. The night has ended, and I'm supposed to be on my way.

His brows raise in question. "You dance, don't you?"

"I dance. I didn't suffer through two years of ballroom dancing for nothing. My mother guaranteed me each time Jimmy Horner stepped on my toes, there would be a payoff later in life."

Damon escorts me onto the dance floor, where he takes control. He twirls and dips me until I'm dizzy. Expecting to stay for a song or two, I'm surprised when he insists we stay longer.

He pulls me close to his chest as the song *'The Way You Look Tonight'* by Michael Bublé plays. We dance in the center of a crowd, yet I feel alone with him in the room. For the next two hours, there is nothing or no one but him and me.

"I think we outlasted everyone here," he whispers in my ear.

When I look around, we're the last couple remaining. The band packs up, and the hotel staff tears down the room.

"I had such a good time, but I'll regret this tomorrow when I have to be up at six for work. For now, I'll bask in the glow of contentment." Sadly, I feel like Cinderella just before the clock strikes midnight. I've just met Prince Charming, but I can't have him.

"I'm glad I met you, and as my mother mentioned earlier, you are a breath of fresh air."

We walk out the front door and down the steps. The car waits, and I expect him to help me in and send me home. I climb inside the car and situate myself. Knowing he'll close the door and I'll ride alone, I remove my shoes from my aching feet.

Damon stands with the door open. He peeks in the car then stands up before stepping back. The door closes, and I feel a sense of sadness as it shuts. Just before the latch clicks, I hear a groan, then the door opens wide, and Damon takes a seat beside me.

"I thought we already said goodbye."

He sits close enough for his body to touch mine from shoulder to thigh.

"Is it okay if I escort you home? I'm not ready to let you go yet." He closes his eyes and rubs his forehead. This is the first time I've seen his confidence waiver. Holding his breath, he releases the air, and his cheeks deflate. "I don't normally do this. I usually just send my companions home by themselves."

"I heard." I rotate my body, so I face him. "I also heard we should have left hours ago, but I'm glad we stayed. It would have been a shame to get all dressed up and not dance with you."

Looking at my discarded shoes, he asks, "Do your feet hurt?"

I chuckle. "I'm certain men designed high heels. They look

great, but after several hours of standing in them, they're like a medieval torture device."

Damon makes room and reaches down to grab both of my feet. He shifts me so that they're in his lap while his long, skilled fingers rub the soreness from my toes. The feeling is divine, and I let out a satisfied groan as he continues to knead his way toward my heels.

"Would you be interested in accompanying me again?" He leans forward, quirks his brow, and smiles.

"Damon, I'm not the escort, I'm the fill-in. I only did this because my best friend needed my help. I'm sure Emma will never double-book again."

"Katarina, I don't want Emma. I want you, and I'm willing to pay you for your time." At the mention of money, he stops rubbing my feet and pulls out his wallet. He flips through his bills and pulls out several hundred. Folding the money in half, he places it in my palm.

The crisp bills feel uncomfortable in my hand. Although they are new bills, they make me feel dirty. Before he can put his wallet away, I hand the money back to him.

Pulling my feet from his lap, I sit next to him. "Thanks for a lovely evening, but I can't take your money. It's just not me. Emma can justify selling her time for money, but it makes me feel wrong. I'm flattered you would like me to escort you again, but I'm not that girl."

His head lowers as he nods in affirmation. "I understand. You're a candy-and-flowers type of girl. You like walks in the park and movies with popcorn. Am I right?"

"You're so good at summing me up in very few words. I wish I were different, but yes, I want the popcorn and movies."

He heaved a sigh. "Sadly, I'm not that guy. Out of curiosity, what are your prerequisites for dating?"

I ponder this for a few moments before responding. "You can't be a serial killer, and you need nice teeth."

"Wow. Nice teeth? Your standards are high, Ms. Cross."

"A girl has to set the bar somewhere." He thinks I'm joking, but nice teeth are important, and he has a smile a dentist would be proud of.

I lean back against the seat and sit in silence for the rest of the trip. Thoughts about how nice dating Damon would be, fill my mind while I leaned against his shoulder and dozed off.

"Katarina? Wake up. We're at your house."

I slowly open my eyes and realize I'm nearly wrapped around his body.

"Oh, I'm so sorry. I didn't mean to fall asleep on you." I feel awful and cheated. I wasted fifteen minutes sleeping when I could have spent them with this man.

"You're exhausted. Work and school can be taxing." He walks me to my door and kisses me gently on my forehead. As he turns to leave, he says, "Call your mom and tell her thank you for the dance lessons. I had a good time." Shoving his hands in his pockets, he looks at the sidewalk. "Take care of yourself, Katarina."

I stand on the porch and watch him walk away and disappear from my life.

Emma opens the door and yanks me in. "Where have you been?" Her voice is almost frantic. "I was so worried about you and thought maybe you had an accident."

"I'm fine. Contrary to your belief, Damon likes to dance. We stayed and closed the place down. He was a perfect gentleman, and I enjoyed myself. Thanks, Em. I never thought I could have so much fun."

With her hands on her hips, she stands before me. "You like him, don't you?" She hasn't been home long herself because she's still wearing the blue dress.

"Yes, I like him, but he's out of my league. I'm not an escort, and I'd have a tough time separating my feelings from my job. How do you do it?"

"I've never connected with any of my clients. And while some are attractive, I feel nothing more than a tingle between my legs."

I blush at her candor, but it is one thing I love about her. She's an open book and always tells it like it is.

"He asked me to accompany him again," I mention.

"Really? What did you say?"

"I told him I'm not the escort, I was the fill-in, and if he needs a companion, he should call you."

"Hmm." She rubs her chin. "I watched you two, and there's something there. You haven't seen the last of Damon Noble. He's into you. Probably wants to get *into* you."

She bursts out laughing, and I wave her off and head to bed. Six o'clock will come much too soon.

CHAPTER THREE

Java Joes at six in the morning is pure torture. Thank goodness it's a Saturday, and things won't get hopping until around eight. Between the lattes and cappuccinos, my mind returns to last night's fundraiser.

Damon Noble is an enigma. He's handsome and rich and charming, yet he hires girls to accompany him to social functions. He could have anyone but remains alone.

There's a story there, but it's one I'll never get to hear. Deep in thought, I walk through my morning on autopilot and help person after person seeing no one's face. They all blend together.

"Hey, Kat. How's it going?" I turn toward the familiar voice.

"Em, what are you doing here?" She hasn't stepped inside Java Joes in over a year because she prefers the little European café down the street. She's what you'd call a coffee snob.

"There's something in my handbag I believe is yours."

"Oh, sorry. I forgot to take out my lipstick and compact, but that could have waited until I got home."

She looks to an empty table in the corner. "Can you sit with me for a few minutes?" She asks, but I know she'll never take no for an answer.

I look over my shoulder at my fellow barista, "Can you handle everything for a few minutes? I have something I need to take care of."

Without waiting for an answer, Em pulls me to the table where we sit down. "What went on with you and Damon last night?" Her eyes fill with questions. I recognize the look as one she gets when she's on a fact-finding mission. Em is like a relentless dog when she's after a bone.

"I told you everything. You were at the dinner and saw what happened." My shoulders lifted. "After that, we danced, and then he drove me home."

Her right brow raises. "It's a huge deal that he did that and coupled with this"—Em slaps down several hundred dollar bills on the table—"I'm intrigued." On top of the bills, she places his business card.

I stare at the stack in shock. Picking up the pile, I count the bills one after another.

"You don't need to count them," Em says. "There's a thousand dollars there, and ... he gave you his card. You should read what he wrote on the back."

I turn the card over and see the inscription.

Best night of my life. Please reconsider.

My lips lift into a smile, and a wash of warmth spreads through me. "I wouldn't accept payment from him. I had such a nice time, and that was payment enough." I stare at the stack of cash. "He must have snuck it in the purse when I fell asleep on the way home."

"I told you he is into you. I could see it from the first moment he saw you. Who would have thought Damon Noble has a soft spot for virginal blondes?"

"I'm not a virgin," I say, a little too loudly.

Every head in the café turns our way, and I die a thousand

deaths while my face flushes red. If I could, I'd crawl under the table and hide until everyone left.

"That one time in the back seat with Kurt Bronson doesn't count," Em whispers. We've been friends since middle school, and she knows everything about me, but just this once, I wish she'd forget about Kurt Bronson.

"Yes, it does, and I did it twice for your information—both times in his back seat, and both times it sucked. I got there with Tommy Mendoza last year, but his mom walked in on us, and he couldn't rise to the occasion after that."

She just stared at me in astonishment, then laughed. "You know, you've just ruined a client for me. He'll probably never call me again. I mean, how will I pay my portion of our rent when you take my paying jobs?" I know she's teasing because of the exaggerated roll of her eyes as she complains. Besides, Em owns the house we live in.

I pick up the stack of money and place it in her hand. "Here's your severance pay. Let that be a lesson to you. Never use me as a fill-in again." I stand to leave, but Em grabs my wrist and places the money in my palm before she turns to leave.

"Oh, no, you don't," she says. "You have to figure this one out on your own. It's your money, Chica, you earned it."

I stuff the wad into my pocket and head back to work.

The last two hours creep by, and by two o'clock, I'm antsy to leave. When the big hand hits the twelve, I clock out and walk the three blocks from work to our bungalow, dreaming of the nap I'll take when I get to my room.

On the doorstep is a large vase of flowers. Em is always receiving flowers from her admirers, and it's not unusual for them to be left at front of the door, so I'm not overly surprised to find them.

Grabbing the large vase, I walk into the house, but as I set the bouquet down, I notice my name is written on the envelope. I pull out the card and read:

Thanks for a wonderful night. Please consider a repeat.

Damon

The romantic part of me wants to swoon, but the smart part of me is mad. Damon Noble thinks I can be bought, rented, or sold. I'll have to educate the stubborn man.

First thing Monday morning, I'll set him straight.

Several hours later, Em and I are sitting on the couch eating takeout Indian food, which is odd because it's a Saturday night, and she's usually booked for some event

"It's not normal for you to be here on a Saturday evening. Why are you home?" My brow raises in question. "Don't get me wrong, it's great you're here, but it's a rarity."

She laughs, "I'll be leaving later. I have a date—a real date." She looks at me, and a Julia Roberts smile stretches her mouth.

"Who are you dating?" Em doesn't date; her choice of employment puts too much pressure on a relationship. She tried once, but the guy got jealous, and it ended badly.

"I'm going out with Anthony Haywood." She sits up. "Am I crazy?" Chewing on her lower lip, she lets it pop loose. "We had such a great time last night, and he asked me to dinner tonight. He's taking me to his new restaurant in Hollywood."

As she talks about him, her voice gets more animated, and it reminds me of when we talked together as kids. We would always sit on one of our beds with some kind of snack food and discuss our crushes.

"Em, that's great! If it feels right, then I think that's great. You know what you're doing." I set my hand on her knee. "Tell me about him."

"He owns restaurants all over the world. His newest is in downtown Hollywood. He's thirty-four and never been married. He's an only child, has a house in Malibu, and I like him. That's all I know."

"I'm excited for you. Since I didn't meet him last night, do I get to meet him tonight?"

"He should be here in about an hour. You know what else I found out?"

"I'm sure you'll tell me."

"He's good friends with Damon. In fact, they're opening a new club together. It's called Ahz, which sounds like Oz, but it is supposed to be the sound of contentment, like in 'ooh' and 'ah.' Spelled A-H-Z. I like it. What do you think?"

"I'm assuming the AH is for Anthony Haywood, and the Z is for Zenith. It's clever."

Her eyes scan the room as she zeroes in on the flowers that arrived today. "You got flowers from Damon?" She cocks her head to the side. "That's another interesting development. I've accompanied Damon to a handful of events, and he has never sent me flowers. I'm telling you, Kat, he likes you."

How she knows the flowers are mine is beyond me. "He is a charming man, but he's used to living his life in a certain way. He hires escorts. He doesn't invest in relationships. No offense to you, but I don't want to be that girl. It would be different if he was interested in a date, but the minute he tossed a thousand dollars at me, I lost all respect for him. I'm not for sale."

"I don't take offense, Kat. I use my resources to the best of my abilities. I bought this house with the money I've made, and I'm not ashamed of what I do."

"You've done amazing things, and I've never once been ashamed of you. Hell, if I thought I could do it, I'd have joined you, but I don't have the backbone you do."

"If I thought you could do it, I'd have recruited you long ago."

"KAT, THIS IS ANTHONY." Em seems like a kid as she introduces her date.

He's a large man with dark hair and eyes that twinkle when he smiles. His hand wraps possessively around Em's waist like he owns her, and she leans into him as if she knows it too. Jealousy threads through me. When will a man look at me that way?

"It's great to meet you, Anthony. Take care of my girl." I walk to the door and watch Em skip down the walkway to Anthony's sports car.

Left alone to my thoughts, I think about Damon and how he held me on the dance floor last night. His strong hands supported my shoulder and waist while he led me around as if he were in control of the music. I'll always remember how it felt to be in his arms, the smell of his cologne, and the feel of his lips as he kissed my forehead.

Depressed, I pour a glass of wine and walk to my bedroom. Sitting on my bed, I look across the room at the flowers Damon sent me. For whatever reason, I can't seem to get away from him. He fills my thoughts, while the scent of his flowers fills my bedroom. I climb into bed and pray that he doesn't fill my dreams.

SUNDAY PASSES like every other Sunday, except Em isn't home. I complete my shift at Java Joes and spend the rest of the day studying for my accounting exam. She arrives home around nine o'clock, walking through the door and falling prone on the couch beside me. Her eyes glaze over, but she looks incredibly happy.

"How was the date?" As if I need to ask. Bliss is written all over her face.

"Oh. My. God. Kat, it was the best night of my life. Before you ask, yes, I slept with him, but it was amazing. I can't remember a time when I've been so satisfied. That man's talents don't stop at cooking." Her arms swoon to land on her forehead. "I didn't want to leave him, but I have classes tomorrow. I just left him, but I'm craving him already."

"Wow." It's all I can say; I've never had an experience like that. My best sexual experience was by myself. My most romantic experience was last night when I felt safe and cherished in the arms of a man who paid me for my time. "When is your next date?"

"Tomorrow night." She giggles. "He's picking me up at six, and we are taking off for a few days to Catalina. I don't have classes until Friday. Do you think you can live without me for a few days?"

"I'm a big girl." I shut my book and shove it aside. "I'm visiting Damon tomorrow to return his money."

"Go easy on him. He's had a tough time of it these last few years." She covers her mouth with her hand as if to stop the information from spilling out. "Forget I said anything. Anthony shared a few things about Damon, but it's not my story to tell. I had no right to say anything."

"You divulged nothing, so no harm done." A tough time? What could be tough about being Damon Noble? He's hot, he's rich, what more could he want? *Me; he wants me.*

"Okay. Just be the sweet, caring, and compassionate girl you always are."

"Damon Noble will never change me."

Em laughed. "The right man always does."

CHAPTER FOUR

The double doors on the Noble building are large and imposing, much like the man who owns the building. Reception guides me in the right direction, and ten minutes later, I am standing outside the corporate office of Mr. Damon Noble, President of Noble Enterprises.

The only thing between him and me is a large door and his secretary. The middle-aged woman addresses me.

"Good morning. May I help you?"

"Hello," I say with confidence I don't feel. "I'd like to see Mr. Noble, please."

"Do you have an appointment, Ms. ...?"

"Cross. My name is Kat Cross, and no, I don't have an appointment, but I'll only need a moment of his time."

Pursed lips show the lines of a woman pushing fifty if not older. Her black tailored suit says she means business, but there is a softness in her eyes that sets me at ease.

"Mr. Noble is unavailable. I can take your information and have him call you when he's free."

I came to see Mr. Noble and had no intention of leaving until I did.

"I'll wait." I needed to get his money out of my purse and back into his wallet.

"You're welcome to have a seat, but he has a full schedule, and I'm not sure when he'll have time to see you."

She's professional and likely telling the truth, but she is getting on my nerves. I smile sweetly at her and say, "I'll wait until he can see me." I look around the posh office space, and when my eyes land on her again, I add, "Even if it takes all day."

"Can I get you something to drink?"

"I'd love some water and your name, please?"

"Certainly, Ms. Cross. My name is Greta." She walks over to a wooden wall and pushes on the mahogany surface. What seems like solid wood pops open to expose a concealed refrigerator and bar area.

Greta reaches in and picks up a bottle of water and a glass, then closes the panel, and once again, the wall appears seamless.

"Thank you, Greta." I take the water and sit directly across from her desk, making sure I remain in her line of sight. Maybe if I sit here and stare her down, she'll accommodate my request more quickly.

Thirty minutes pass. Forty minutes pass. An hour goes by.

I'm well into my second hour of waiting when Greta's eyes dart to her phone. She picks up the line and responds. "Yes, Mr. Noble. Will there be anything else?" She glances in my direction, and I look at her with pleading eyes. "Mr. Noble? There is a young woman by the name of Kat Cross who has been waiting to see you. She doesn't have an appointment, and I've informed her that your schedule is tight. Will you be able to make time for her, or shall I schedule an appointment for another day?" There is a pause as she listens for his answer. "Yes, sir," she replies. Greta hangs up the phone and walks over to where I'm seated. "Mr. Noble will see you now."

"Thank goodness. I appreciate you letting him know I was here."

She irons the wrinkles from her skirt with her palms. "Please, follow me."

At the door, she raps lightly before opening it and swinging the door wide for me to enter.

The whole time I sat waiting, I never felt nervous, but seeing him again makes my insides shake. There's an undercurrent crackling just below the surface, and I can't decide if it's fear or anticipation.

Damon rises from his chair and is at my side in seconds flat. He leans over and places a chaste kiss on my cheek. The innocent little peck makes my heart race.

He takes my hand and leads me to a soft leather couch.

He holds up his hand. "Don't go anywhere. I'll be right back." He walks to the door and exits.

I didn't realize I was holding my breath until my chest hurt. I release a whoosh of air and follow it with an inhale to bring oxygen to my deprived brain.

Damon Noble will be the death of me. I can't breathe or think when he's around.

"Sorry to keep you waiting, Katarina. I didn't know you were here. I promise that won't happen again."

Oh, why can't he be the dating type?

Dressed in a tailored blue pinstripe suit, he is a sight to behold. From his perfectly trimmed hair to his hand-polished shoes, he is the ideal specimen.

"The wait wasn't a problem."

"I'm so pleased you came to visit me." His smile is warm and welcoming.

"Thanks for seeing me on such short notice. I came to give you your money back. I told you I didn't want compensation for my time. Friday night was the best, and I don't want to cheapen it by the exchange of money. Please consider our time together a gift."

I pull the thousand dollars out of my purse and put it in his palm.

He frowns and places the money on the table to the right of the couch before sitting down beside me. His nearness causes my muscles to tense, and my breathing to accelerate.

"I wanted you to have the money because I valued our time together. I'd have left more if I'd had it in my wallet, but that was all the cash I had on hand. If I had treated you like a normal escort, I'd have handed you three hundred dollars and sent you on your way."

A sigh pushes past my lips. "Damon, the exchange of money makes me feel like a whore." There, I said it, and he looks like I slapped him in the face.

"How could you feel like a whore? I asked nothing of you except to see me again." There is hurt in his eyes, and I can't figure out why he'd feel wounded when I'm the one he treated like a prostitute.

"I can't explain it. You acted like the perfect gentleman, and I almost forgot you were paying me to be with you." I shift so that I can face him, and our knees skim one another. "If I could get rid of the money exchange, it would have seemed like a date." The heat from an innocent touch threatens to burn me alive. "You told me I'm pure, and in some ways, you're right. I'm not as forward-thinking as I thought. Really, I'm an old-fashioned girl."

"I get that." He rubs his chin, the slight scruff sounding like sandpaper against his fingers. "But I'm not a dinner-and-movies kind of guy. However, I can offer you lunch. Greta ordered something for us, and I hope you'll stay."

I want to stay, but I also want to run as fast and far away as I can. Damon Noble spells trouble with a capital T. The curious side of me remains. I mean, I sat patiently and waited for two hours to see him, so the least he can do is buy me lunch.

Greta wheels in a cart that smells delicious. Sitting on top of an elegant teacart are two covered plates.

Damon takes over the presentation, dismissing Greta and

leaving us alone. On the coffee table in front of me, he places the plates and lifts the lids with a Bobby Flay flourish.

Pieces of grilled salmon, steamed vegetables, and rice pilaf are artistically displayed on white china. It almost seems a shame to eat it.

He pulls a napkin from the cart and lays it on my lap, then walks to the bar against the wall, and fills two glasses with diet soda and ice.

"I ordered salmon because you enjoyed it so much the other night. This was delivered from Anthony Haywood's. They do a great job and are my go-to when I can't escape the office for a meal." He takes a seat beside me and hands me a glass. "It's how I met Anthony. We've known each other for years." He pulls the soda to his lips and takes a drink. "I understand Emma and Anthony are dating." He looks at me for confirmation, but with my mouth full of salmon, I can only nod yes. "I never thought he'd find anyone who could tame him. They make a nice-looking couple, don't you think?"

"I've only met him one time, but they look nice together, and Emma seems taken with him."

"What about you, Katarina? Is there someone special in your life?" He appears genuinely interested in my response, though I can't imagine why.

"No. I'm single. How about you?"

"I rarely date. In fact, I have a strong personal policy against it, but there is one woman I'm attracted to. Unfortunately, she doesn't seem interested." He toys with me.

"Maybe she doesn't understand you. I mean, if you offered her money to be with you, then she'd think it was a business transaction, but if you ask her out, she may consider a date."

"Is that right? I'd have thought the compensation would be a clincher for most girls. I have to admit, I'm rusty on the dating scene, but heard women were attracted to money and flowers and all that nonsense."

I stabbed a piece of broccoli and held it in the air. "There's your problem. You think romance is nonsense, and with that attitude, you'll never get a date. As for money ... I make my own and don't need a man for that."

"Maybe it's in her best interest to stay clear of me. I'm a mess and can't offer her what she needs."

"You'll never know until you try, but that would require some of that romantic nonsense you're averse to."

Damon faces me and takes my hands in his. "Can I try something? It's just an experiment, but if it goes the way I think it will, then you and I will have a longer conversation. If you feel nothing, then walk away, and I'll leave you alone."

In the next instant, his hand wraps around the back of my neck and pulls me toward him. Soft lips brush mine as his velveteen tongue coaxes my lips apart.

I feel something that travels from the tip of my head to my toes. It's heat and need mixing with excitement and desire. The kiss deepens as our tongues mingle, and a muffled moan slides up my throat only to be swallowed by him.

Seconds later, Damon breaks our connection. "Tell me you didn't feel that." His eyes bore into mine as he waits for my answer.

"Oh, I felt something all right, but I think it was your tongue down my throat." I smile at my attempt at humor.

"You wound me." He places both of his hands over his heart. "I've been told I'm a good kisser. Have I been lied to?"

"I have so little to go off of. Maybe I could sample another kiss to make an educated decision."

He needs no further enticement and possesses my mouth completely. The passion in his kiss is overwhelming, and I'm forced to shove against his chest to break the seal. The moment his mouth leaves mine, I regret pushing him away. If I could only learn how to breathe around this man, I'd sit and kiss him all day long.

"And the verdict is?" he asks.

I waffle slightly before I answer. "Whoa. You can definitely kiss. I don't think my toes have curled from a kiss before."

Damon smiles and pulls me to his chest. I inhale the scent of him while he gently rubs my back. "You are unique among the women I've met—so open and honest."

"I don't know if I should relax in your arms or run for the door. Being here excites and scares the hell out of me at the same time."

Squeezing tighter, as if to hold me forever, he says, "You're a smart girl, Katarina, and you should run for your life, but I hope you stay."

My decision is made when I melt against him, and the tension releases from my body.

He sinks against the sofa back and holds me in silence until the intercom buzzes.

Greta's voice breaks the tranquility to inform Damon that his two o'clock appointment has arrived.

"I have to take this meeting." He looks at me with hope. "I can pick you up for dinner tonight at six if that works for you."

With a nod of my head, I walk with him to the door. He steps aside to let me pass, and I feel the weight of his gaze as I exit his office and skip all the way to the garage.

CHAPTER FIVE

After a forty-minute drive home, I enter an empty house and race for the shower. "I'm having dinner with Damon Noble!" I scream.

In my addle-minded state, I never asked where we were going, and don't know what to wear. The weather is pleasant enough, and my royal-blue maxi dress will have to do. I leave my hair down and apply light makeup. Damon seems to like that I'm authentic, so tonight there's no ball gown and professionally applied makeup. What he sees is what he gets—no bells and whistles.

With twenty minutes to wait, I grab Emma's copy of *Bound*. Armed with the book and a diet soda, I sink comfortably into the couch and read.

Time passes quickly as I lose myself in the story, and when the doorbell rings, I earmark the page and set the book down in the center of the coffee table.

I answer and find Damon dressed in slacks, a button-down shirt, and a sports coat. He looks upscale casual. He follows me into the house.

"Let me get a sweater, and I'll be ready to go."

His eyes run the length of me, and as he looks at my face, a smile unfolds—first in his eyes, then on his lips.

When I return from my room, I find him sitting comfortably on the couch with the book in his hands. There's a look of fascination on his face as he flips through the pages.

"It's Emma's. I was passing the time. Have you heard of it?" I ask, slightly embarrassed to have him find a sex-filled novel on my table.

"Who hasn't heard of it? It's been a number one seller this whole year. Are you reading it?"

With a shrug, I say, "Yes. I started it this afternoon while I waited for you to arrive."

"And?"

"So far, it's entertaining. What's most intriguing is that Friday, you made a comment that was like one I read in the book."

"Really? What was it?"

"Something about having unconventional tastes. I got the impression we weren't talking about ice cream or creme brûlée."

"You're a perceptive woman. Don't worry about my specific tastes. I don't gravitate toward floggers and hot wax, but I'm open to suggestions and experimentation if that's your desire. We can discuss our specifics at dinner."

Surprised by his response, I shift from foot to foot. "I can assure you I do not long to be tied up and tortured."

"I don't know, a little bondage could be fun." He appears to enjoy this exchange. It's as if my discomfort entertains him. "Shall we go? I made reservations at my favorite Italian restaurant. Do you like Italian food?"

"I love it. Do they have good lasagna?"

"The best I've ever had."

We drive in Damon's silver Mustang to a restaurant called Tony's, where we're ushered to a corner table toward the back of the dining room.

He helps me into my seat and sits beside me rather than across from me. It's a small place with red-checkered tablecloths and pictures of various Italian landmarks like the Tower of Pisa and the Trevi Fountain. Garlic floats through the air mixing with the sound of Frank Sinatra and clinking plates.

"If you take your wallet out to pay for anything besides dinner," I say, "I'll beat you. Do you understand?"

"I think you've been reading too much of that book I found on your table." His hand covers mine. "I won't guarantee that I won't pay for things, but I promise I won't offer to pay for your time tonight. Can we agree to that?"

"It's a start. Now let's order dinner before I get hangry."

"We can't have that." He flags down the waiter, and we order a starter and our meal.

The restaurant fills with people as we nibble on antipasto salad and calamari. A soft murmur of conversation surrounds us as we talk about mundane things like the weather.

"What do you think of the food?" He wipes his mouth and sets his napkin on the table. "I found this place several years ago, and it's my go-to for authentic Italian."

"It's amazing. Just the right amount of garlic on everything. Sometimes you go to these places and taste the garlic for days—no one can stand to be around you, but this is great. Thanks for inviting me."

All throughout dinner, Damon and I unconsciously take turns staring at one another. His blue eyes pierce mine, and I melt for him.

"Tell me about your family, Katarina. I want to know everything about you."

"There isn't much to tell. I'm the second child of Mike and Marion Cross and have an older brother named Chris. Yep, I know—don't say it. He caught a lot of crap for having the name Chris Cross even though the duo spells their name Kris Kross." I raise my hands in the air and sing Jump. This causes a giggle as I remember how much shit my brother got because of his name. "My dad is an accountant, and my mom is a stay-at-home wife. Chris is a loan officer for a large bank. We grew up in Arcadia, where my parents still live in my childhood home."

"What were you like as a teenager? What were your hobbies?"

"I was like most teens. I had big dreams and limited potential, but I grew into myself. High school track kept me busy, and I still run several days a week. My college graduation is in May, and I hope to find a job as an event planner. I'd also entertain the possibility of being in management, but I don't know if I have the skills to lead a group of people. Seeing you today at your office was inspiring because you're so confident and capable. How do you make it look so easy?"

"It's more about the people you surround yourself with than anything else. I hire capable people, and they do their jobs well. You should contact our human resources department. They may have an opening in your area of expertise. I'm co-branding with Anthony Haywood, and we're ramping up for the grand opening of Ahz."

"Emma said something about that. You're so young and have accomplished so much. I want to know more about you, Damon."

He hesitates for a moment as if deciding what he wants to tell me. I can see the indecision in his eyes until he exhales and speaks.

"You met my mom. She's on the board of directors at the hospital and has spent her life dedicated to finding a cure for cancer. My father died from lung cancer when I was a young boy. I was twelve when he passed." His fingers tap on the table. "I made my original investment money from being a DJ. I spent my youth in clubs and paid attention. I developed a successful business model and opened my first club when I was twenty. Now I'm twenty-nine, and I'm expanding into other territories." He lifts his hands in the air. "The rest is history. There are nineteen Zeniths across the world. Only two are outside of the United States. One is in London, and the other is in Paris. I grew up in Brentwood, live off Mulholland Drive, and went to UCLA like you."

"Are you an only child?"

"I am now," he says. His voice short and stilted.

I don't respond, because I hope he elaborates. I believe a person should be able to tell as much or as little as they feel comfortable. I'm not a person to pry, even though I want to know so much more about Damon.

He cautiously considers his next sentence. "I had an older brother who died from leukemia when I was twenty."

I reach out my hand and place it over his. "I'm so sorry. That must have been awful."

"More so than you can imagine, but it was a long time ago. Let's talk about something else."

"Okay, why don't you date? You're a handsome man with a charming personality. Fill me in."

"I have had the pleasure of escorting many beautiful women to various places, but I don't do the dating thing. I can't make the commitment it requires to maintain a healthy relationship. There isn't enough time to do it all, and I've got other priorities."

It's the other things that are his problem. Everyone can make time to build a friendship, but something tells me Damon is not sharing everything, and that's okay, that's his prerogative.

"Would you like dessert?" he asks.

My mind is elsewhere, and I barely register his question. Shaking my head, I try to clear the errant thoughts from my brain. "What?"

"Would you like dessert?"

"Um ... no, I'm good."

"Coffee, then?"

"That I'll have because I have a test tomorrow and will undoubtedly stay up late studying."

We sit tucked in the corner of a tiny Italian bistro sipping coffee.

Damon drinks his black while I take mine with a dash of cream. Not enough to make it white, but enough to cut the bitterness.

"Thanks for having dinner with me tonight." He turns his cup round and round on the saucer, then stops and pins me with a questioning look. "Can we talk about earlier?"

I play dumb and pretend like I don't know what he's talking about, although I know it's the intoxicating kiss we shared in his office.

"What are you referring to?"

"You can't sit here and pretend we don't share a physical attraction. Kissing you is like being hit by a train."

"Is that supposed to flatter me? If so, you need to work on your wooing."

"A lovely woman once told me flattery will get me nowhere."

I made a pfft sound. "She was crazy. Flattery from you might get you somewhere."

He placed both hands flat on the table. "Herein lies the problem. I want to see you again, but I can't give you what you want." He moves one hand to take mine in his. "I enjoy the time we spend together. You make me feel something I haven't felt in years." Looking into my eyes, he asks, "What would it take for you to consider seeing me regularly? Not dating, but something we can mutually agree on."

I sit at the checkered table, shocked. This man can't possibly be that stupid. I mean, he runs a multimillion-dollar company for God's sake.

Pulling my hand from his, I respond, "We're back to a business transaction?" My heart plummets to the pit of my gut. "I'm not interested. You're a nice man and an excellent kisser, but I'm not for sale or rent." I toss my napkin on the table. "I'm ready to leave if you're still willing to take me home. Otherwise, I'll have the restaurant call me a cab."

"No, I'll take you. You should study and get rest before your class tomorrow."

I nod in agreement. What an idiot I was to think I could have someone like him. I don't know if I'm angrier with myself or Damon.

He helps with my sweater, letting his hand linger on my bare arm while he slides up the sleeve. A buzz of energy runs through my body where he touches me. Reaching up, he pulls my hair out of the sweater, so it hangs loosely around my shoulders. With his hand placed firmly at the small of my back, he walks me outside and helps me into the car.

We drive in silence all the way to Emma's house. Once we arrive, I throw the door open and dash up the long walkway to our front door. I've had enough of Damon Noble for the night.

But his long legs give him an edge as he catches up with me. Reaching out, he grabs my arm and spins me around to face him.

"Wait. It doesn't have to be like this. We could see each other, go out to dinner, and attend various functions, then you could quit your job at the coffee shop and invest time in your studies. It's a win-win."

"Nothing about that scenario is a win for me. You get what you want, and I get a new boss. I trade my time for money and my soul for time with you. I like you, and I think there is definitely something between us that could have been explored, but we have different needs. I can't give you what you want, and you won't give me what I need. I'm sorry."

Looking at him, I see understanding in his sad eyes. Resignation is written all over his face.

The tall, proud man gets smaller with every step he takes back to his car. He stops at his door and glances my way before he climbs inside and drives off.

ice

CHAPTER SIX

Em returns from Catalina on Thursday. Her skin is tanned to a golden brown, and her hair lightened to a strawberry blonde, but the most notable change is her eyes, which are bright and happy.

"Oh, Kat, I think I'm in love. You wouldn't believe what I experienced in Catalina." She flops on the couch in front of me. "We stayed in a house by the seaport, sailing by day and snuggling at night. He cooked every meal for me. There is nothing sexier than a man in the kitchen." She gushes nonstop, then asks, "How did your meeting with Damon go? Tell me everything."

I sit next to her, turning my body to face her. "Nothing happened. Just the normal stuff, like school and studying. I returned his money, we had lunch and dinner, and then he propositioned me again. He wants to rent me regularly. I told him no."

Her eyes bug out at my statement. "He didn't!" Em knows me like the back of her hand and seems as appalled as I am.

"He did." I nod in affirmation. "Listen. He's a complex man who kisses like a master, but I can't settle for so little when I know I'd want so much more. There's no reason to set myself up for such a disaster."

"Wait, I'm still at kisses like a master. You kissed him?" Em's eyes looking for a clue to what I'm not telling her.

"Yes. I kissed him twice in his office. The first was an experiment, and the second was to confirm my belief that he's an excellent kisser." A sigh deflates me. "When somebody kisses you like he kissed me, something happens to your insides. My toes curled, Em. I couldn't survive too much of that and then have him dismiss me when he grew tired of me. I wouldn't be able to stop my heart from getting involved."

"It sounds like you've given it a lot of thought." She looks mildly disappointed. "Too bad, because we could have double-dated."

"Speaking of dating, what are you going to do about your escort service? How is Anthony going to respond when you dress up and accompany other men to various functions?"

"We talked about it, and I decided I'm closing up shop for the time being. He's okay with me doing what I do, as long as I promise not to wear the blue dress." She laughs. "He has claimed that dress for his eyes only." A dreamy look blankets her face. "After giving it thought, I couldn't imagine spending time with any other man. All I'd be thinking about was Anthony."

"We have three months of school left before we graduate. I always planned to quit after graduation, anyway. It's time to find a real job. My savings account is solid, so I can afford to be out of work for a while." Her fingers twirl a strand of her hair as she talks. "Speaking of graduating, Anthony mentioned they have temporary job opportunities at Ahz. The opening will be huge, and they need all the help they can get. You should apply. Besides, it would give you experience, and it's an excellent resume builder."

"I'd be afraid of running into Damon." While Ahz is a perfect fit for my degree, being in the same building as Damon would drive me crazy.

"I'm sure you would never run into him. It's a large corporation that employs hundreds of people. You could get lost in the crowd."

"Damon told me about the positions when we had dinner, but I'm still hesitant to apply."

Emma is right. I'm sure I wouldn't even see him, but if I did, I'd thank him for suggesting I apply for the job, then I'd move on.

"Thanks, Em. You are right, I should apply."

"Do it right now before you chicken out."

I give her a hug, grab my laptop from the table, and head to my room.

The application process is thorough but straightforward. I apply for an internship as the assistant to the event planner, press send, and close my computer. With nothing else to do, I head to the kitchen to make a cup of cocoa and pick up Em's copy of *Bound* on the way. With cocoa in hand, I collapse onto the soft, overstuffed sofa. A few minutes later, I hear the beep of a text coming in.

Hi, it's Damon. I am hoping maybe we could be friends in some capacity. Are you having a nice night, Katarina? What are you doing?

I think about his question. Could I be friends with him? I suppose there's no harm in being nice, so I text him back.

Damon, if you're going to be my friend, then you have to call me Kat. All my friends call me Kat. Right now, I'm drinking hot chocolate and reading Emma's naughty romance novel.

I picked up a copy for myself today. I wanted to see what all the women are talking about. What page are you on?

That's interesting. I'd never have imagined you to be a fan of "girlie" books. I'm on page 57.

I'm learning you can find out a lot about women from a "girlie" book. I should have been reading these all along. I'd be so much smarter when it came to the fairer sex if I'd paid attention from the beginning.

Don't get pure entertainment mixed up with what girls want.

Take this book, for instance. The protagonist is a young college graduate who meets a charming man while doing her friend a favor. Doesn't that sound familiar? He wants to see her on certain nights, and he's willing to pay her. Wow, that's sounds familiar too. Where the story differs is she says yes and well ... you know the rest.

This is a book about exploring different avenues for sexual satisfaction. When I was a boy, you could only find stories like this in adult magazines. It seems to be mainstream these days. That's what the sexual revolution has done for us.

Since I haven't read that far, I'm not sure where this is leading, but with a title such as Bound, I'm guessing we're headed to the kinky side. It's not my normal genre. I like sweeter romance novels, like the ones where the man comes racing in on a white stallion and saves the day. Emma tells me this story will get way out of control.

What about you, Kat? Do you like being out of control?

How do you mean? Are you talking about restraints and gags, or something different?

No, just your average scarves or a pair of fur-lined handcuffs. No Saint Andrew's Cross or dungeon cages.

Holy shit. The man gets straight to it.

I haven't given it much thought. If I'm being honest with you, and I feel one should be honest with their friends, then I find the idea intriguing. I definitely would not want my mouth gagged, but being restrained could be fun. You would have to have some agreement as to what you're willing or not willing to do.

Check out page 87 and text me back.

What am I doing? I feel like I'm in a book club for the deranged. I put down the book, refusing to be tempted to see what lies ahead. Then I think about restraints, and then I think about Damon *and* restraints. My body reacts at the thought of being restrained in front of Damon, and I wonder what he would do. I can't resist the temptation, so I pick up the book and flip to page 87.

Oh, holy hell. I can't believe what I'm reading. The agreement is long and comprehensive. Many of the things he wants to do to her are foreign. I open up my computer and type in *seahorse triple action*. The picture that shows up is shocking. I'm stunned by the sheer size of it. Oh ... my ... goodness! People can get inventive.

I slam my computer closed and put the book on the table. My cheeks flush as heat courses through my body. My phone beeps with another incoming message.

Well?

I lie.

I haven't read it, so I don't know.

Didn't you tell me that one should be honest with friends?

Leave it to him to throw my words back at me. I type out the longest text ever.

Yes, I did, and you've caught me. I'm uncomfortable talking to you about this book. I read it, and I'm quite appalled. I had to look up one device, just to see what it was. It comes in several speeds, widths, lengths, and colors. What happened to good old regular sex?

People have different tastes. This book describes a particular flavor, but there are many out there. Where have you been hiding?

I haven't been hiding. I just haven't been experiencing too much of what other people are tasting.

I could present you with a buffet of experiences to try. What do you say?

Good night, Damon.

I put my phone down and mosey my way to my bed. Laying my head against the pillow, I think about Damon and how he'll be the death of me.

CHAPTER SEVEN

I wake to the sound of my ringtone—a cacophony of birds chirping. They are loud enough to hear and unpleasant enough to want to answer immediately.

"Hello."

"Can I speak to Katarina Cross, please?" the woman asks.

I sit up and try to sound wide awake. "Yes, this is Katarina."

"This is Della Fields from Noble Enterprises, and I'm calling about the internship position. I have your résumé in front of me, and I'd love for you to come talk to us about the opening we posted."

My heart rate picks up its pace, but I control my excitement and tell her in a calm and professional voice, "That sounds great. What day and time would work best?"

"I know it's last minute, but can you be here at one o'clock today?"

"Absolutely." I hop out of bed and start dancing around my room. "Where do I go when I enter the building?"

"Someone at the reception desk will guide you to the human resources department."

"Perfect, I'll see you then." I hang up the phone and jump into the air, waving my arms in celebration. It's only an interview, but it means one of two things. I have the skills they are looking for, or they are desperate and need warm bodies. Either way, it's a job opportunity.

Another option enters my mind. Did Damon have anything to do with me getting the call? The idea is silly since I just filled out the application last night. I can't imagine him even knowing I applied for the internship. I dance across the hall to tell Emma.

"I've got an interview at Noble Enterprises!" I scream in delight as I sashay around her room.

"What time is it?" she grumbles and pulls her duvet cover over her head to shield her from the sun peeking through her window.

"It's nine o'clock, and everything is all right in the world, Em. Get up and have coffee with me, and then help me find the perfect interview outfit." I dash from her room to the kitchen to make us both a cup of coffee. I slam every drawer and cabinet to make sure she doesn't fall back to sleep. "Don't forget, you owe me big, and I'm taking my payment now. Get up!"

Em appears in the kitchen in her flannel pajamas and bunny slippers. She slides into a seat at the table and circles the coffee mug with both hands, before she brings it to her lips. I know she needs that first sip to jump-start her morning.

"Okay, so what time is this interview?" she asks.

"It's at one o'clock, and I want to make an impression. It's an internship position for Ahz. I'll work with their event planner."

"You know, Kat, I'm familiar with both owners. I can put a good word in for you." Her head rests on her arm, which stretches across the table. I know this girl, and she'll need another cup before she's any use.

"No, I want to do this by myself. I could call Damon, but I won't because it's important to earn my successes. Besides, I'm trying to avoid him. Let me tell you the latest." I top off her cup and sit across the table from her. "He bought *Bound*, and he's reading it." I pause for dramatic effect. "He texted me last night so we could discuss it. It's as if we were in our own private book club. We texted about bondage and vibrators."

Em stares at me with a look of confusion on her face, then bursts out laughing. "I don't know what's funnier, you talking about vibrators, or Damon reading an erotica novel. I have to give that some thought." Sipping her coffee, she adds, "At least the conversation is happening via text. Could you imagine having dinner face to face and talking about the latest Rabbit that hit the market as you ask him to pass the bread?"

I hadn't given it much thought, but Em is right. Texting allows us to be honest and bold with our answers. As open as I am, I'd never have had that conversation in person.

As if talking about him summoned a text from him, the familiar beep of my phone redirects my thoughts.

Only read to page 125. I'll call you at seven o'clock tonight to get your thoughts.
Damon

I ignore his text and focus on my upcoming interview. Em drags me to my room, where she chooses a fashionable but conservative-looking skirt, a silk blouse, and low-heeled pumps. She advises me to wear my hair down, explaining that if I wear a ponytail, I may look too young, and if I pull my hair up into a bun, I may look too haughty. I trust her because she has never steered me wrong.

I stand in front of her for her final approval.

"I'd hire you," she says with a wink.

Reaching forward, I give her a big hug and a smooch on her cheek before I dash out to my car.

The forty-minute drive to Noble Enterprise seems like seconds. Once inside, I'm directed to the fifth floor, where I check in with the secretary. Within minutes, I'm led into a large office where Ms. Fields stands up from her desk to greet me before offering me a seat.

She shuffles a few papers sitting haphazardly on top until she finds the one she's looking for.

"I see you are in your last semester at UCLA, studying hospitality management. Looking at your schedule, it appears you are available Mondays and Fridays any time and Tuesday through Thursday in the afternoons. Is that correct?" she asks.

Della Fields looks to be in her early forties with brown hair that's pulled into a severe knot at the back of her neck. The style mixed with her black and white suit gives her an air of authority. If the quality of her clothes is any indication, Damon pays his people well.

"Yes, that's right, although I'll graduate soon."

"Why Noble Enterprises?" she asks.

"Honestly, Ms. Fields, I'm looking for a chance to get a little experience in my field of study. A friend told me about the job opening, and I applied. Ahz is the perfect opportunity for me to use my education and learn from a seasoned professional."

"Why should I choose you?" Della questions.

"There's no reason for you not to choose me. I'm motivated, educated, and ready to work. I'll give you one hundred percent every day."

She sits back and twirls the pen in her fingers. "I'd like you to meet our event planner. His name is Trevor Thornton."

Ms. Fields presses the intercom button and asks the receptionist to have Trevor come down to her office. A moment later, a tall man with wavy brown hair walks inside. "Trevor, this is Ms. Cross. She's applying for the intern position."

He offers his hand to shake before he greets me. "Nice to meet you, Ms. Cross. Ahz is a unique challenge for us. It's the first time we'll combine two concepts. What do you bring to the table that other applicants don't?"

"That's a good question, and my best answer is I bring an open mind with no preconceived notions of what the job should be or what the final project should look like. I hope to learn from you. I'll adopt your vision and strive to help you accomplish your goal." Happy with my answer, I take a breath and wait for a response.

Ms. Fields and Trevor exchange looks. A hint of a smirk lifts his lips.

"Thank you for coming in today. You're our final applicant. Give us time to compare notes, and we'll get back to you. The candidate we choose will be expected to start immediately. Is that an issue?"

"I could start today if you needed me."

"We'll let you know." Ms. Fields closes the door behind me, and I let out a whoosh of air.

Wow. That was an interesting interview. It was direct and to the point.

I exit the office and see a familiar silver Mustang parked in the spot closest to the elevator. I didn't see it on my way in, but I was focused on the interview. Seeing the sports car makes me think of Damon and the night he took me for Italian food.

I wish things could have turned out differently.

EM ACCOSTS me as soon as I get home. "Tell me about the interview. How did it go?" I think she's more excited than I am. Or maybe, she's had too much coffee.

I toss my keys and purse on the table near the door and collapse on the couch. "It went well. I met the event planner. His name is Trevor. He seems like an experienced guy, and it would be great to learn from him. He's done an exceptional job marketing Zenith under Noble Enterprises."

"When will you know?" She prods me for additional information.

"I hope within the next day, but who knows. I have to wait and see, I guess. Let's celebrate anyway. What about tacos?"

She rolls her shoulders forward and frowns. "I can't. Anthony is picking me up. He's cooking me dinner at his house."

"Gosh, Em, it sounds like things are getting serious, fast."

"Yeah, I guess, but we are so compatible. It's pure magic."

"I'm thrilled for you. I've never seen you look so happy."

"Oh, Kat, I feel like I'm walking around in a dream that I never want to wake up from."

ANTHONY PICKS Emma up at five, leaving me on my own for the night. I have a texting date with Damon at seven that I'm looking forward to.

Too lazy to go out for tacos on my own, I change into my old comfy jeans and make myself a bowl of instant macaroni and cheese, then curl up on the couch to read.

Turning to my earmarked page, I try to catch up, hoping to get to page 125 before he texts. I'm lost in the book when my phone rings.

"Hello," I say.

"Hello, Katarina. This is Della from Noble Enterprises."

Oh, my God, my heart beats as fast as a hummingbird's wings. "Ms. Fields. How are you?"

"I'm well. I'm calling to offer you the internship. Can you start tomorrow after your classes? Your first day will be all paperwork. You'll start work with Trevor on Friday."

I dance around the living room as Della Fields gives me the details. Once I hang up the phone, I shout joyfully from the top of my lungs.

Holy smokes, I have a paid internship at Noble Enterprises. They're paying me double what I make at Java Joes. I immediately call my current boss to let him know about my new opportunity. I agree to work the weekend shifts until he can replace me.

At exactly seven o'clock, my phone rings. I expected a text from Damon, but I guess he decided on something different.

"Hi," I answer.

"Hello, Kat," he responds. His pronunciation of my nickname comes out with a nasally twang, making it sound unattractive. I think he does this on purpose.

"Aren't we texting?" Although I'm glad he called because I miss hearing his voice. He has a strong, commanding tone that I find incredibly sexy. I guess you could say I'm a traditionalist when it comes to relationships. I expect a man to act and sound manly.

"I wanted to hear your voice. Is it okay that I called?"

How sweet is that? "Yes, it's okay."

"I'm in your area, and I don't want to eat alone. Will you join me for dinner? As a friend."

"I just ate a delicious bowl of instant macaroni and cheese," I say.

"Oh ... okay." The disappointment in his tone is obvious. "I thought maybe if you hadn't eaten, we could eat together."

"Well, I haven't had dessert, so ... how about I have something sweet while you have something savory?"

I don't know why I offer to go. Maybe it's because I can't stand for him to sound disappointed. And if I'm being honest with myself, I want to see him again.

"That's great," he says excitedly. "I'm just around the corner and will be at your doorstep in a moment." His tone went from sullen to ecstatic in a heartbeat.

Seconds after I hang up the phone, he knocks on my front door.

I swing it open. "Wow. That was quick. Should I worry because you were so close to my house?" I ask him teasingly.

He laughs. "I hoped you'd say yes, but if you didn't, I'd have driven past your house and gone home. I don't have stalker tendencies." His eyes glide over me. "You look great."

"Thanks." I take him in from his loosened tie to his Italian leather shoes. "You, too. I see you're getting used to my nickname."

"It doesn't roll off my tongue easily, but I respect your wishes, even though I prefer to call you Katarina."

Looking down at my jeans and cotton T-shirt, I say, "Let me change into something nicer."

Without waiting for an answer, I turn and head toward my bedroom. His grip on my elbow pulls me back.

"You look amazing the way you are. There's no need to change. Let's go to the Asian restaurant up the street. If they don't have a good selection for you, I'll take you someplace else."

Once I slip into shoes, he walks me to his car and opens the door. He's always a gentleman, and I never tire of his good manners.

At the restaurant, he orders a combo platter while I get deep-fried banana wontons with caramel sauce and ice cream.

"Now that we're here, let's talk about the book," he says just as they deliver the food to our table.

The mention of the book makes me blush. Texting about it is one thing, but talking about it face-to-face is different.

"I haven't completed the pages I was supposed to read. As you can imagine, I'm busy with school and stuff."

"You're blushing, Kat. Surely, two friends can discuss a book." He says this with a straight face, but there's mischief in his eyes. He knows this makes me uncomfortable, and he gets something out of it, which only makes me want to rise to the challenge.

"Certainly," I say, not willing to let him get the best of me. "I'm on page one hundred fifteen. She signed the contract and agreed to a limited term as his mistress. He insists on full control while he employs her." I cut my wontons in pieces. "Why would someone give up so much? What's in it for her?"

"There's the money, but ultimately I think she wants to relinquish control. Her character is organized and tidy and somewhat OCD. That takes a lot out of a person. To have someone else decide for a while might be nice for her. It's also the only way she can be with him. And her need to be with him is stronger than her need to be independent." He places a piece of broccoli in his mouth.

"Hmm. I don't think money plays any part in it. I agree it's the only way she can be with him. The attraction between them is stronger than anything she's felt before." I lick the ice cream from my spoon and set it down. "On some level, I think it's bold of her to allow herself to be vulnerable."

Choking on his food, he takes a sip of water before continuing. "Why does being with him make her vulnerable?" He places another forkful of food into his mouth and chews while waiting for my response.

"He's introducing her to a world she is unfamiliar with. It takes courage to step out of your comfort zone."

He nods. "Yes, it does. When you accompanied me to the hospital benefit, you were out of your comfort zone, but you did it for your friend. It turned out well for your friend, and I think you enjoyed it, too. Am I correct?" His eyes watch me intently.

"I had a great time. It was one of the most memorable nights of my life." I look at him and see a flash of relief pass. It would appear that my happiness matters to him.

"Sometimes, what may seem out of the ordinary can become something pleasurable."

"I can't argue with that." I pick up a deep-fried wonton dripping with melted coconut ice cream. "Who would have thought banana wantons could be this good?"

Damon laughs. "What do you think of his particular tastes?"

"Well, short of the contract that talked about various sexual activities, some of which I had to look up on the web, I haven't arrived at the point where his depravity presents itself."

"Why is it depravity? You like bananas, but I detest them. Does it make us distinctively different because we have different preferences? Am I a worse human for not liking bananas?"

I think for a few minutes and conclude he's right. We all have different likes and dislikes, and just because I don't share someone else's desires, doesn't make me better and them worse. "I agree with you. It's okay as long as both parties are willing."

"She signed the contract."

"Yes, she did, but I wonder if her judgment is clouded by her attraction to him." Didn't that sound familiar?

"That could be, but she seems like a bright woman."

We sip our tea in silence. I think about the resemblance between the characters in the book and my story with Damon. Thank goodness I jumped off the train before I got too far along.

"I had a great time. Thanks for coming out with me on such short notice. We killed two birds with one stone. We got to discuss the book and eat. Shall we make a habit of this? Just two friends, having dinner and discussing a good read?"

Part of me wants to say yes, but the sane part knows I should say no. Too bad that part never wins. "Yes, on one condition. We take turns paying for dinner. Next week, I'll choose the place, and I'll pay, but you can still drive. Let's keep Wednesday open for book discussions."

He's visibly excited to negotiate a weekly Wednesday date.

Wait, this isn't a date. It's more like a book club meeting.

"Perfect. Same time next week, then? I'll pick you up at seven."

He pays the bill and takes me home. He walks me to my front door and waits until I open it. Chivalry is not dead.

Before turning to leave, he bends over and brushes his soft lips against my forehead. I'm certain he'll give me another one of his panty-twisting kisses, but sadly, he doesn't. I set the rules, and he's playing by them.

CHAPTER EIGHT

Thursday afternoon, I fill out paperwork and watch safety videos. Friday, I arrive at eight o'clock and meet Trevor on the third floor, where the public relations and advertising offices are located.

He takes me on a tour of the building, but thankfully we avoid the executive offices. I don't want Damon to know I'm working for his company. It's important for me to have an authentic experience, one that won't be changed by his influence.

Trevor sits down with me and outlines the grand opening plans. The official party will take place on June fifteenth. The complex features ten bars within six distinctive environments. Ahz includes three ultra-modern dance floors complete with state-of-the-art audio and visual enhancements. It hosts a ninety-foot stage for live musical performances, a modern VIP lounge, and a rooftop terrace offering spectacular skyline views.

The first floor has Anthony Haywood's. The fifth floor contains the VIP lounge. Floors two through four make up the live performance venues. The sixth floor is rather unique. It has a glass floor so the people in the VIP lounge can see everything that's happening above them, and vice versa. Trevor plans to take me on a tour of the entire building next week.

He outlines my duties, which means I'm basically the go-to girl for everything no one else wants to do, and I'm okay with that. I'm excited to be here, soaking everything in like a sponge.

Trevor gives me his background, telling me he went to school back east and has been working for Noble Enterprises for five years. He has successfully opened over half the clubs for Zenith with the most recent opening in London.

"How was working in London?"

"It's different from opening a club here. We always open with a top-rated performer, and they always have specific things they require. In London, we opened with an American band. Have you heard of Mystic Mavens?"

"Yes, they're not my cup of tea, but they have a huge following."

"They also have huge egos, and here's where we come in. It's our responsibility to secure the act, but we also have to make them happy. That's the biggest challenge. Mystic Mavens were impossible." He grumbles something unintelligible. "They insisted on American-made products. They wanted special drinks and special foods, special lotions, and specific toilet paper," he explains. "We paid them an extravagant amount of money, yet they continued to make demands. They wanted gift bags in their rooms that contained everything from L'Occitane to Cartier. I had to charter a private plane to deliver everything they required, and we had to pay a fortune in import taxes."

"Wow. That must have been pricey. What did you learn from the experience?"

"I learned I should hire a local band," he says as he laughs. "In the end, the opening was a success, and the London location is one of our most profitable sites."

"What's the key to your success?" I have three months to learn everything I can from him, so I'll ask questions until he turns blue from answering me.

"I think it's all in the details. The big things are easy. Booking the entertainment is the small stuff. It's everything that happens in between the concept and opening day that matters." Shifting in his chair, he continues. "You need to know everything that's happening in the world. If there is a caviar shortage, you don't want to have it on the menu for your grand opening. If your guest of honor is allergic to nuts, don't serve baklava. Anticipate everything and everyone's needs. That way, you won't get caught unprepared."

"Who is the opening act for Ahz?" I ask.

"That will remain a secret, but it will be the biggest thing happening in the Los Angeles area this summer. I'm going to have you help me come up with gift packages for our VIP guests. We need one hundred gift bags, and your budget is one thousand dollars."

"I have to make one hundred memorable gifts, and I only have a budget of one thousand dollars?" My voice sounds panicked.

"You have a budget of a thousand dollars for each gift." Trevor shows me to the cubicle I'll use during my internship. "There's a list of previous sponsors on your desk. Sometimes companies will donate their products to get exposure. Feel free to call any of these sponsors and or companies you feel would benefit from an opening like ours. I imagine the value of each gift bag will range between five thousand and ten thousand dollars when it's all said and done." He rises from his chair and walks to the door. "I'm heading out for the rest of the day. I want you to work on the gifts. I'll meet you here on Monday at eight o'clock so we can take a ride to Ahz. Have a great weekend, Kat."

I feel overwhelmed with the major undertaking he assigned. Sitting in front of me is a list of over one hundred sponsors, from Tiffany's to Oakley. I look over the various companies and place stars next to the places that make sense. I want these gift bags to mean something. Anything having to do with dining, music, entertainment, or food stays. I place all other products on a secondary list. Companies like Tiffany's and Pandora stay on a maybe list. They may have items that fit in with the theme, like a cool charm or key chain. I'll contact them if I need anything additional for the bags. Within an hour, I have reduced the list to fifty potential companies.

Two hours later, I have placed calls to twenty-seven of them. Seven have guaranteed a donation, and I'll follow up with the rest on Monday. I'd love it if I didn't have to spend anything on the gift bags. If I could get everything donated, I could save the company a hundred thousand dollars. It's probably a pittance to a corporation as large as Noble Enterprises, but I'd feel a great sense of accomplishment if I could do that. It would also look great on my resume.

Clocking out for the day, I take the stairs to the garage. I try to avoid places where I might run into Damon, and since his offices are on the top floor, I imagine he takes the elevator each day. Five flights of stairs several days a week will give me a good workout, as well as keep me out of sight.

"HEY, Kat. How was your first real day at work?" Em calls from the kitchen as I walk in the front door. Something smells amazing, and I hope she's made enough for two.

"It was so good. Trevor is a great guy. He was thorough and made me feel comfortable." I inch toward the stove to see what's in the pot she's stirring. "I avoided Damon, so that's a plus."

"Will you ever tell him you're interning at his company?"

"Not if I can help it. I don't want him interfering in my experience. I don't want to get special treatment because I know him." I look over her shoulder. "Is that spaghetti I smell?"

"Yes, are you hungry? I made a bunch. I'm taking some to Anthony's, but there's plenty for you to enjoy."

"I'm starving." Taking a seat at the table, I watch Em finish making dinner. "Make sure Anthony says nothing to Damon. Okay?"

"I didn't tell him you got the job." She hands me a bowl of pasta sprinkled with parmesan cheese.

The scent of oregano and Italian spices rise with the steam. "Thanks, Em. It's great having you home."

She gives me a wide smile before I dig into the big bowl of happiness.

Fed and satisfied, I move to the living room and sit down on the couch with my copy of *Bound*. Wondering where Damon is in the book, I send him a text.

I'm trying to catch up to you. What page are you on? How is it a man as busy as you has time to read frivolous materials?

He responds immediately.

So, the beautiful Katarina is chasing me, so to speak. I'm on page one hundred and fifty. I won't go any further so we can be on the same page for our Wednesday night meeting. Where are we going?

I think Mongolian BBQ. Will that work for you?

Can I call you? I hate texting long messages.

Yes.

Seconds later, my phone rings, and I answer with a slow, soft, "Hello, Damon."

"Hello, Kat, how was your day?"

"It was good. You know, the same old stuff—school and work."

"I thought you didn't have school on Fridays?"

Oh, shit, I almost blew it and try to salvage my mistake. "No school today. Just a bunch of research." It's not a lie. I called a lot of companies regarding donations. "What about you?"

"Things are moving fast with Ahz, and the closer we get to the grand opening, the more frantic things become."

"What about Anthony? Is he helping?"

"His staff is pulling their weight. Em has been helping with marketing on the Anthony Haywood side, but it's still a lot of balls to juggle. Everything is moving in the right direction." He stalled for a minute. "Would you like to come to the grand opening?"

I'm floored by his invitation. It's the biggest thing happening this summer. Would I like to attend? Duh!

"I'd love to come, but I'm sure you have more important people to invite."

"There is no one I'd want to invite more than you. I'm sure Emma will accompany Anthony, but if she doesn't, I'll get her an invitation. Oh, by the way, my mom asked about you and insisted I bring you to Sunday dinner. I told her you work and probably couldn't come, but I'd be a bad son if I didn't pass on her message."

"Your mom invited me to dinner?"

"You impressed her at the fundraiser, and she wants to enjoy your company in a relaxed environment. We try to meet up for a meal once a month, and this Sunday is our day."

"I'm flattered, but I don't want to interrupt family time with your mother."

"Please, come and save me from my mother's monthly dating inquisition."

"Are you begging me?" I imagined him in front of me on his knees.

"Will it help?"

"I like being in this position. It makes me feel powerful."

"I wouldn't have pegged you as a dominant."

"I don't see myself that way, but I'm open to new experiences."

"Is that right? You know, I'm happy to teach you anything you want to know."

"Are we still talking about dinner?"

"We are. What else would I be referring to?" His deep, full laugh makes me feel warm from my insides out.

"Pick me up at Java Joes at five."

"My mom will be ecstatic."

"What about you?" I'm playing with fire by teasing him. I know it's not wise, but it sure is fun.

"I'll rejoice with her. See you Sunday. Dress casually."

"See you." I hang up feeling joyous.

For the next fifteen minutes, my thoughts are all on Damon. I close my eyes and envision his physical attributes and imagine his tall, slender body, broad shoulders, narrow hips, and long legs. I can see his dark hair, blue eyes, and his soft, supple lips ... oh, those lips that make me lose all thought. Yep, Damon Noble is trouble—big trouble—for me.

SATURDAY FLIES BY, but Sunday drags on. I look at the clock for the tenth time that hour and swear it doesn't move. This time with Damon is all I've thought about since Friday night. Though we spoke last night, too, the conversation was short, and I hung up wanting more.

The clock seems to move backward as I busy myself by cleaning the espresso machine and stocking supplies for the next shift. With a damp rag in my hands, I turn around to wipe the counters and find the Viking god leaning against the wall, staring at me. He's always watching me.

"What are you doing?" I ask him.

"Waiting for you to get off work. Can I get a coffee to take with me?"

"Geez." I toss the rag into the sink behind me. "You'd think this was a coffee shop," I say teasingly. "What's your poison, Mr. Noble?"

"A plain-brewed coffee will be perfect. I'm a simple man."

"I find that hard to believe."

CHAPTER NINE

I take advantage of the twenty-minute drive to Brentwood to study Damon's profile. His hair parts from left to right, leaving the bulk of it sweeping toward me. The blue of his eyes is the most vivid color of blue imaginable—the color of an Alaskan glacier.

His nose is well-proportioned—not too big, but not dainty. There is a slight bump near the bridge, suggesting he'd broken it previously. His chin is strong and covered with a shadow of whiskers darker, redder than the rest of his hair.

"You better stop looking at me like that." His lips curl into a smile as he delivers his warning.

"Like what? You're driving. How can you know how I'm looking at you?"

"I can feel your eyes on me and makes me think of doing things to you that friends don't do to one another."

I whip around and stare out the windshield.

Damon breaks out into a laugh that causes me to giggle.

"You're an awful friend. A good friend would never have said anything."

"A good friend wouldn't visually strip me while I drive to Brentwood."

A gasp comes from my mouth. "I wasn't doing that." I lifted my chin in defiance. "I only got as far as your lips."

"I stand corrected. You may resume your inspection."

"What happened to your nose?"

"What do you mean, what happened to my nose? My nose is perfect."

"Yes, it is perfect for you, but you've broken it before. Remember, I have an older brother, so I recognize the injury. Chris had his nose broken twice. Once skiing, and once in a fistfight. What's your story?"

"My brother Roman broke my nose when I was thirteen. I borrowed his favorite baseball mitt and lost it at the ball field. My dad had given it to him, so it was special." He heaves a sigh. "I spent the next four days sitting at the ballpark, asking everyone who showed up if they found a mitt. I'd about given up when a mom and her three kids arrived in a minivan." He risks a glance in my direction, then turns back to the road. "I almost didn't ask her but figured it couldn't hurt. She went around to the back of her van, reached in, and pulled out my brother's mitt. It was one of the best days of my life. Roman always felt bad for breaking my nose, but it was a good lesson for me. It taught me to never take what's not mine."

Just as he finishes his story, we arrive at his mom's Brentwood estate. To call it a house would lessen it. We enter through a security gate and wind along the driveway to the magnificent Tuscan villa. In the center of the circular drive sits an Italian fountain that sputters water from three different levels.

"Did you grow up here?" I ask with a touch of awe in my voice.

"No, Mom bought this house about six years ago. She entertains a lot, and the house suits her needs. It's over the top, but she's paid her dues and deserves it." Damon points in the direction they came. "My childhood home isn't far from here. It's a traditional house that sits on a large lot." The hint of a smile curves his lips. "Our dad built Roman and me a tree house in the largest oak tree I've ever seen. It wouldn't surprise me to find that tree house still standing in a hundred years."

As he talks about his brother, a range of emotions cross his face. Everything from happiness to sorrow and something in-between. His eyes say everything without saying a word.

He escorts me to the front door, where his mother greets us.

"Katarina, I'm so glad you came. Damon said he didn't think you could make it, but I was positive you wouldn't disappoint me. Come in." She stood aside so we could pass. "Let's have a drink before dinner. What can I get you?"

"A glass of wine if you have it." I follow Rose to a beautiful hand-carved bar where she pours Damon and me a glass of wine.

Rose takes the only single chair available, forcing Damon and me to sit next to each other. His leg presses to mine from thigh to knee. Goose bumps rise on my skin.

"Tell me what you've been up to since the fundraiser, Katarina?" Rose asks.

"Mom, she likes to be called Kat." He looks at me and smiles.

"Nonsense," Rose says with conviction. "Katarina is a lovely name. Why would you shorten it?"

I scowl at him and see merriment dance in his eyes. He seems to say, "I told you so."

"It's just a nickname. You can call me, Katarina. My mom fell in love with the name when an ice skater from Germany won the gold medal in the 1984 Olympics. As far as what I've been up to lately ... just the normal stuff, like school and work."

"You work in a coffee shop in Hollywood? That must be an interesting place to watch people."

"Katarina is good at watching people," Damon says, looking into my eyes.

I silently return a message that tells him to behave.

"It's so nice to see you two together," Rose comments with glee in her voice.

I don't want her to get the wrong impression, so I correct her. "Oh ... no. We are not together. We're just friends."

"Some of the best relationships begin with a solid friendship."

"Mom, leave it alone," he groans.

"Oh, shut up, Damon. Let your mom dream. Katarina, do you know how difficult it is having a wealthy son? I can't hold his inheritance over his head to get my way. What's a mother to do?"

"Behave," he admonishes.

Rose rises. "I'll check on dinner. Help yourself to the wine."

As she leaves the room, Damon and I stand to stretch. He takes our glasses to the bar and tops them off while I take in the beautiful furnishings and art.

The fireplace mantel catches my attention. A lifetime's worth of photos is spread across the marble surface. Damon reaches around me to hand me my glass and remains close, leaning over my shoulder. His breath caresses my neck while he walks me through the photos.

The pictures tell the story of the Noble family, starting from the left to the right, the tale begins. A beautiful wedding photo of Rose and her husband starts the journey. Damon's dad's name was Simon, and he was a biology professor at USC. The next few pictures are of Roman, and then there are pictures of Damon. Roman was two years older than Damon and had similar features. Comparing the brothers, I'd say Damon was the better looking of the two.

Turning to face him, I sing his praises. "Look at how cute you were. I bet you broke a lot of hearts with those eyes."

"I was never the heartbreaker, but always the brokenhearted." His vacant look makes me wonder where he went. It's obviously a place that's painful to visit.

"That's hard for me to believe. I call you the Viking god, and can't imagine the girls not falling at your feet."

"Viking god?" He grins. "I like that."

Caged between his body and the fireplace, my heart pounds at the excitement of his nearness. It's useless to lie to myself. I like this man.

Instinctually, I reach up on tiptoes and kiss him quickly. It's a peck, really. Barely a pass by, but the action shocks both of us.

He hops back, and I bolt for the safety of the couch. We part just in time for Rose to call us for dinner.

He leads the way to the formal dining room, where the kitchen staff serves Cornish game hens.

"Katarina, next Saturday is a benefit for Roman." She slices into her chicken and sets the bite aside. "Every year, the Los Angeles Philharmonic performs, and all proceeds go to the Roman Noble Scholarship Foundation. Roman played piano with the Philharmonic for two years before he passed away. Every year, we raise enough money to help several budding musicians go to college. I'd be honored if you'd join Damon and me on Saturday. It could be fun."

Damon groans before he tries to reel in his mom again. "Mom, she doesn't want to come to the performance. She most likely has plans."

Something about him dismissing me drives the conversation. "I love the Philharmonic and would happily join you. Should I meet you there?"

Rose bounced in her seat. "Excellent. Damon will pick you up or send a car. Won't you, Damon?"

He pastes on a smile. "I'd be delighted to pick you up." He appears pleased, despite his phony smile.

They ate their dinner where interspersed conversations about the weather, Katarina's classes, and the opening of Ahz were discussed between bites.

"Let's have coffee in the living room."

We sit on the couch and wait for Rose to return with a tray of cups and a pot of coffee.

"This will be so much fun. What do you think you'll wear, Katarina?"

"I don't know. I don't have much formal wear, but I can borrow a dress from my roommate." I turn toward Damon. "What about the blue dress Emma wore at the hospital fundraiser?"

Damon lets out a groan, and I laugh.

We stay another thirty minutes before we say our goodbyes.

Damon's mother has the heart of a lion.

"Thank you for a great night. Your mom is nice," I say.

"She likes to have her way. I'm sorry you got roped into going to the Philharmonic on Saturday. Hopefully, your preparations won't interfere with book club."

"I don't see why it should," I answer.

"Speaking of book club ... I bought you a gift." Damon reaches into the back seat and hands me a rectangular box.

I open it. "A scarf?"

"You'll understand."

"So, this has something to do with the book?"

"Most assuredly, and as a side benefit, it's silk and soft and beautiful," he says

"Now I have to stay up and read."

Twenty minutes later, we're sitting in the car parked in front of my house.

"Kat, I wanted to say something about the kiss tonight."

"I'm sorry. I had a moment, and I reacted impulsively."

He opens his door and rounds the car. When he reaches my side, he pulls me out a little too roughly, causing me to stumble into his arms. Before I register another thought, Damon's lips are on mine. It seems like hours before we end the kiss that makes me feel weak in the knees.

"I've been wanting to do that all night." He breathes in through his nose and out through his mouth. "Can I come in for a few minutes? I'm not ready to leave you yet." His eyes are downcast, so I tip up his chin to look into them, but all I see is uncertainty. Odd for such a confident man.

"That would be nice."

We enter the empty house and make our way to the couch. In a matter of minutes, we're a tangled mess of limbs and lips. I feel like a teenager.

Damon slows the pace and kisses me leisurely. His tongue delves deep inside my mouth, and when he pulls back, he sucks in my lower lip, only to devour me again.

He leans back and licks his lips. "I've got to go." Damon stands and dashes for the door.

I chase after him, but he's halfway down the sidewalk before he turns and says, "See you Wednesday."

What the hell just happened?

CHAPTER TEN

Monday morning, I dig right into my donation requests and land the hottest leather bags available. They'll be the perfect container for all the goodies I'll get.

After a few more calls, Trevor rushes in. "Kat, I'm so sorry I'm late. We were supposed to be out of here an hour ago for the tour. Grab your stuff, and let's go."

With my sweater in my hand and my purse over my shoulder, I run after Trevor, who has legs twice as long as me. I'm barely in the car before he takes off.

He races through traffic and gets us to Ahz in record time. It doesn't matter that my stomach sits in the heel of my right boot or my heart beats like I ran a marathon, we're here, and no blood was shed.

He races into the building and stops in the middle to take a breath.

"The restaurant will be here on the first floor," he says on an exhale. "The rest of the floors are entertainment venues." He points to the wall at the back. "The elevator is over there. Why don't you take a self-guided tour, and I'll catch up with you?"

Floor by floor, I go until I'm in the VIP lounge. The place is dark and plush with comfy groups of seats everywhere, but it's the tall booths surrounding the room that intrigue me. They're private enclosures, big enough to sleep on, and I can't resist the urge to try one out.

Lying on the velvet sofa, I stare at the ceiling. The lights above come on, and I watch people walking above me through the glass flooring.

Holy smokes—I can see everything. My imagination takes off, and visions of dancing bodies fill my head. There are scantily clad women with their hard-body partners swaying above me. I think of several girls I know who are averse to panty lines and giggle at how exposed they'd be walking across this floor. Looking up a girl's skirt from this room could get you an eyeful. Damon must have been having naughty thoughts when he came up with this design.

I visit the glass dance floor and keep to the tiled sides, so I don't flash my utilitarian, white, cotton undies today.

An hour later, Trevor finds me on the rooftop terrace, where he talks about his vision for opening night, and I update him on my gift bag progress.

"You're killing it," he says.

I smile because he's right. I am killing it. This job was custom made for me.

THE NEXT TWO days go by quickly as I work on various projects for Trevor and attend classes. Damon and I talk every night, but neither of us brings up the kisses we shared Sunday.

On Wednesday, I hurry home to get ready for my date. I know it's not a real date, but I can't stop thinking that our time together is more than what we tell ourselves.

Unfortunately, with my new schedule, I'm behind with my reading. With a good half hour before he arrives, I read the next several chapters.

Holy Moses, now I know why he gave me the scarf. If his intent was to stir emotion, he gets an A-plus.

Two can play at his game. Dressed in a low-cut T-shirt and jeans, I take the scarlet silk from the box and tie it loosely around my neck. What a great reminder of the bondage chapter.

The roar of his Mustang rattles the windows as he pulls up in front of the house. I rush out the door with the book in my hand and hop into his car.

"I would have come to the door for you, Kat."

"I know, but I'm so excited to talk about the chapter. I think our discussion will titillate, don't you?" I play with the scarf, wrapping it around my wrist repeatedly.

"You're doing that on purpose. Stop it, or we won't get to dinner." His tongue slips out of his mouth to moisten his lips, and all I can think about is how much I want to suck that tongue into my mouth.

"So many threats, and so little action," I tease as I roll my tongue over my lips, mimicking him.

His eyes widen, and a soft murmur that sounds like hmm comes out.

MOON MONGOLIAN BARBECUE is the perfect location for tonight's talk. The chapter was descriptive, and I'm sure I can make him squirm. He seems to enjoy making me come unhinged, so let's see if I can turn the tables.

We both head to the buffet to fill our bowls with various meats, veggies, and sauces. While we wait for our food to grill, I reach for my silk scarf and weave it around both of my wrists, raising my hands above my head to grab his attention. I keep twisting the ends until I'm bound.

"Is this what you had in mind?" I whisper. "The fabric is soft, yet so strong."

Damon lunges forward and unwinds the scarf from my wrists and places it back around my neck. "Be careful, Kat. You don't want to go there. You don't know what you might unleash." He bites his lower lip and lets it pop free. "I'd have no problem tying you up right here in front of everyone."

Shocked, I step back but never stop playing with the soft fabric.

His expressive eyes track my every move. I think about his threats and convince myself they are simply that—empty threats.

Once we have our plates of food, we walk to our table and start tonight's book club meeting.

"What's your take on this week's read?" I ask.

"Well, last week we discussed their good looks and how that might influence them. Do you still think that's the case?" He eats a forkful and looks to me for an answer.

"I think their attraction to each other draws them together. Combined with the pure sexual chemistry they share, it's addictive, but it goes deeper than that. She cares about him and wants to please him because she wants to be everything he desires."

"Don't you think being someone's everything is taking it too far?" he asks.

I debate the question for a minute or two. "You can lose yourself in a passionate romance, but there's a way to navigate it and remain true to yourself."

"How far would you go for a person you cared about?"

"I'm not sure. I've never been tested that way. I see the main character's perspective. She cares for him, and she also knows he'll take her to places she's never been, but it scares and intrigues her. Why do you think he insists on the contract?"

He glances from side to side, then looks at me before saying, "The exchange of money keeps feelings out of the equation."

I move the broccoli around my plate. "Is that why you hire escorts? Are you afraid of emotional attachments?"

His head snaps back like I splashed him with ice water. "We're not talking about me. We're talking about the book."

"I think we may be talking about both."

"I'm not up for discussion tonight. And on that note, I think we're done for the night. Ready to go?"

I'd hit a nerve with my comment. Rather than pick at a scab, I pay the bill, and we leave the restaurant.

Once we are back in the car, he reaches into the back seat and pulls out a large box. "This is from my mom. She thought it would look nice on you." He sets it in my lap. "You shouldn't have to borrow a gown for Saturday, especially that blue one." He taps the box. "If you don't like it, you don't have to wear it."

"Tell your mom thank you." I'm floored his mother sent me a dress for the performance.

As we pull up in front of my house, I wait for him to come around and let me out. I'm not letting him off the hook tonight.

He dismissed me at the restaurant, but I won't let him ignore me now.

He walks me to my door like he's walking to a hanging—his. Before he can turn around and leave, I drop the box and pull him to me for a kiss. I give him everything I have to offer in that kiss; my loyalty, affection, and maybe a piece of my heart.

He doesn't respond at first, but as I part his lips with my tongue, he gives in and kisses me in return. His passion pours into me, and I have no doubt that he feels something for me.

"I care about you," I whisper against his neck as I settle into a hug.

"You shouldn't." He gently pushes away until our eyes connect. "I'm not good for you."

"Let's take it one kiss at a time, okay?"

He shoves his hands in his pockets and looks down at the ground like an uncertain kid. "I'll see you Saturday at six."

I pick up the box, close the door behind me, and watch him walk to his car and drive away.

"What's in the box?"

I jump several inches at Em's voice.

"Shit, Em! You scared the living daylights out of me."

She looks out the window at Damon's fading taillights. "I see things are moving forward with Mr. Noble. That was quite a kiss on the porch."

"Were you spying on us?"

She was because Em doesn't like to be the last to know about anything.

"How else am I going to find out what's going on around here?"

I move to the couch and set the box on the cushions. "You could stay home occasionally, and then you'd have the 411."

She reaches for the box top and flips the lid off. We both look at the ice-blue gown carefully placed within the tissue. I pull it out and let it unfold. It has a round scoop neck and beading that goes all the way to the floor with a slit that rises to mid-thigh. The color is familiar, it's the same as Damon's eyes.

"Did he buy you this dress?"

I hold it up to me and turn around. The beaded fabric feels heavy in my hands, but it's too beautiful to put down.

"No, his mother picked it out and thought it would look nice on me. I'm attending the Philharmonic on Saturday with them to pay tribute to Roman."

"Hmm. Now you're dining with the parent. Wow, you move fast." She touches the scarf hanging around my neck. "Where did you get this?"

"Don't you miss anything?"

"Nope, but I can figure out the connection. First, it's the book, then the scarf. It sounds kinky."

A shiver runs up my spine. "You have no idea."

"I might," she says. "Listen, Anthony and I are going to Catalina on Friday, and we'll be gone until Sunday. I worried you might get lonely, but now that I know you'll be with Damon, I feel better about leaving."

"Even if I didn't have plans, I'd be all right. This is my last weekend at Java Joes, so things won't be so crazy." I set the dress back into the box and run my fingers down the beads. "How are things going with Anthony?"

A big smile spreads across her face. "It's almost too good to be true. Things are dreamlike. What about you and Damon?"

"Damon is … complicated. He's convinced he's bad for me, and he keeps cautioning me, but I see something good in him."

"Just be careful, okay? If someone likes you enough to caution you about themselves, you should at least consider their warnings."

"I will."

I give her a big hug and take the dress to my room.

I feel like Cinderella on her way to the ball.

CHAPTER ELEVEN

Thursday and Friday pass without a word from Damon, but it's no surprise with the way he acted the other night.

One minute he's playful, and the next minute he's distant. I don't understand what to make of it, so I let him have his space. Not knowing if he's still picking me up for the concert, I send him a quick text.

Are we still on for tomorrow? I need to know if I should make other arrangements for transportation.

Within seconds he texts back, confirming he'll arrive at six. That was it. Just a verification. No hello. No how are you? Nothing.

Saturday zooms past, and I rush home after work to shower. I have less than an hour to put myself together. Just as I'm applying my lipstick, the doorbell rings. I hop on one foot to the door, trying to put my other heel on, on the way. When I open the door, Damon is there looking delicious in his tuxedo. It's hard to stay upset with him when he takes my breath away.

Calm down, heart.

I take a few deep breaths and regain my composure. "I'm almost done. Come in. Let me get my bag, put on my earrings, and I'll be ready."

He steps through the door and waits while I rush around, looking for Emma's silver shawl. I find it on my dresser and wrap it around my shoulders before rushing back to the living room.

"You look stunning," he says. "The color and fit are perfect on you."

"I wonder how your mom knew."

"It must be a girl thing." His eyes smile like he has a secret. Offering his arm, we walk to the waiting limousine.

A sense of déjà vu washes over me. Was is only weeks ago that I sat in this same limousine with him? He's in the same place, staring at the slit of my dress as it rises up my thigh.

"You must have had a busy week." I don't want to pry, but I'd like to know why he didn't call. His silence for the past two days feels like a punishment.

"Things are always busy," he says.

He's pulling away from me, and my heart aches. My hope was he'd see me in this beautiful dress and want to hug or kiss me, but he didn't.

He sits stiffly in the seat across from me and stares at my legs until we reach the venue, and the driver opens the door.

People surround Rose, but she notices our arrival and waves us over. Being the gentleman his mother raised, Damon guides me to her before stepping away.

With a look of satisfaction, Rose announces I'm perfectly dressed for the event.

"Where did you get that dress? It's beautiful."

"Damon said you sent it." I look over my shoulder to find him, but he's not there.

"It's not from me. He must have picked it out." She touches the beading at my shoulder. "He has impeccable taste, don't you think?" She smiles with pride.

"You raised him well." Shock addles my brain. What's the deal with him? He buys me this amazing dress and then keeps his distance. I don't understand what message he's trying to send. Does he want to be with me or not?

He walks up with two glasses of champagne.

I lean in and whisper, "Thanks for the dress. It's beautiful."

He smiles warmly and whispers back, "No one but you could wear that dress. It was made for you."

I'm touched by the sincerity in his voice but confused by his immediate disappearance into the crowd.

I sip my champagne and mingle with Rose. A handsome gentleman approaches, and Rose introduces him as Russell, an anesthesiologist at the hospital where she works. Russell lifts my hand and places a lingering kiss there. Embarrassed, I tug it back and turn away.

Off to my right, Damon stands with a scowl intimidating enough to scare the devil himself. He looks at Russel and then at me before he walks away—again.

Rose does her best to introduce me to every sexy, single, and successful man in the room like she's trying to set me up, while Damon just stands at the perimeter looking apoplectic.

"All this attention you're getting isn't sitting well with my son."

I feel his penetrating eyes on me. The heat from his fiery gaze is like lava on my skin. "I don't think he cares." I lie.

"Oh, he cares, and this will teach him to not leave you alone." Rose bursts into a fit of laughter as she moves toward their private box. "Something rare is always desired, but it's the smart man who claims it first. Let's see if tonight puts a flame under my son's ass." She takes another look at Damon and snickers. "Shall we, Katarina?"

Rose is not someone I want to anger because she doesn't play fair.

THE PERFORMANCE IS WONDERFUL, the company is lovely, and my champagne glass is never empty. During the intermission, Damon broods in the back of the box while his mother occupies me every minute.

When it's time to leave, I realize I'm drunk. Rose and I giggle as we totter our way to waiting cars. Damon climbs into the car next to me, and I immediately reach for a glass and the decanter of wine.

"Do you think you should drink more, Katarina?" The sarcasm drips from his voice.

"Oh, you speak?" I lift the decanter into the air. "I probably shouldn't drink more, but I will because what could have been the best night of my life, got ruined by you." I fill my glass full and lean over to slurp the top so that I don't spill.

"Me? Do you think you could have talked to any more men? You made it through the whole audience. All that was left was the orchestra, and given enough time, I'm sure you would have charmed them too."

"I talked to others because you didn't talk to me." I take a big gulp of wine. "What does it matter, anyway? I don't belong to you. You don't date, and a man who doesn't date can't claim a woman." I toss back my glass of wine and pour another. "What's wrong with me? Am I so awful you can't stand to be near me?"

He leans back and rubs his eyes. "Nothing's wrong with you. You're perfect. If I could give you what you needed, I'd sweep you up and keep you, but I'll never be that man."

"Can't, or won't? There's a difference," I say coldly.

He sits in silence and watches me toss back two more glasses.

I barely register the car stopping and Damon telling the driver to wait. My body moves, but I don't know how. Cool air brushes my face when I get outside. My feet don't hit the ground, which means I'm in Damon's arms.

I trace his lips with my finger. "Your lips are mind-blowing. You don't know what they do to me, but when we kiss, my body erupts."

My words slur, but he hears me. "I had big dreams for you, buddy, but you're impossible," I poke at the knot of his tie. "I could love you, but you keep pushing me away. Tonight, I wanted to climb into your lap and have you hold me." Sighing, I continue. "But you couldn't get far enough away from me. I know in my heart you'd be worth the effort. Too bad you don't see your potential." My head flops to his shoulder. "The girl who wins your heart will be the luckiest girl in the world."

My head spins, or maybe the room spins. Either way, I close my eyes, and the last recollection I have is him kissing my lips and telling me I'd have won his heart if he had one to give.

CHAPTER TWELVE

The next morning, I wake to my alarm and a massive headache. The last thing I remember was leaving the concert. I was furious with Damon, but everything after I entered the car is vague.

I'm not sure how I got into my house or undressed and into my bed. I had to be in better shape than I thought because my dress hangs nicely in the closet, and my shoes and jewelry are in their place.

Needing to quell the headache, I drag myself to the kitchen, and on the table sits a note with two aspirin and a glass of water.

Sorry,

Damon

In a flash, it all comes back.

The ride.

The wine.

My confession of love.

Things are unclear after that, but deep down, I know he undressed me and tucked me into bed.

I press my hands to my aching head and moan. I need time to get over this headache and the regrets that come with it, but I have to suffer through it to complete my final day at Java Joes.

When I get home, I'll climb in bed and stay there until Monday morning.

A MORNING HUDDLE with Trevor starts the week before I chain myself to my desk to work on the gift bags. The watches I worked on getting are now a guarantee. So far, the gifts range from spa days to Cristal Champagne. I wait for word on the chocolates and silk scarves I requested.

Thoughts of silk scarves bring Damon to mind.

Redirecting my musings, I inventory the things I received. There are bags, books, videos, CDs, watches, hotel stays, Anthony Haywood gift certificates, and so much more. The value sits at close to six thousand dollars for each bag, but I'm reaching for ten.

Trevor walks to my cubicle and asks me to follow him upstairs for a company meeting. On the tenth floor, human resources is giving a safety seminar.

We file into the large room where at least three hundred people sit waiting. I find a space in the least conspicuous place and focus on the seminar about network security. It lasts less than thirty minutes and bores the staff to death. I half expect to see Damon, but relief floods through me when I don't.

After the meeting, Trevor gathers the team and invites us to a working lunch. We crowd into the elevator and hit the first floor in seconds.

The doors slide open, and Damon's voice bounces off the walls of the lobby. I hear him before I see him. There's no avoiding him. As he steps into the elevator, I exit it.

"Kat?" He stands in front of the door so it can't close. "What are you doing here?" Concern colors his voice. "Is everything okay?"

I call ahead to my group and tell them I'll catch up.

With a smile that sits like an imposter on my face, I say, "I work here. I took your advice and applied for the internship."

"Why didn't you tell me?"

"I wanted to do it on my own. Besides, you haven't been talkative lately." My coworkers walk out of the building. "Gotta go, people are waiting for me." I dash after them to catch up with Trevor and the others.

"I'm sorry about that," I tell Trevor.

"How do you know Mr. Noble?" He lifts a quizzical brow.

How do I explain my relationship with Damon? Without a clue, I divulge as little as possible. "We were in a book club together, but he quit because of a conflict."

"I don't see Damon Noble as a book club kind of guy. What books do you read in this club?"

This is like a college exam I didn't study for. "Mostly books on The New York Times Best Sellers list." I change the subject to avoid further discussion. "Where are we having lunch? I'm starving."

"There's a diner down the street that has the best burgers in town."

We spend an hour eating and discussing the grand opening while I gobble up something called a black and blue burger.

Once the lunch meeting concludes, we head back to Noble Enterprises.

As soon as I arrive at my cubicle, my phone rings and Greta asks me to come to Damon's office. It's not a surprise since I didn't give him a chance to react to my presence.

Greta greets me with a smile. "Hello, Ms. Cross. It's a pleasure to see you again. Mr. Noble is waiting for you."

She raps twice on the door and opens it a crack. There's a murmur from inside, and the door swings wide open.

"Thanks, Greta," I cautiously walk into his lair. That's the only description that comes to mind because, at the moment, I feel like a mouse entering a lion's cage.

"Come in, Kat, and have a seat." He waves toward the couch. "I'll be with you shortly." He nods to a tray with soda. "Help yourself to a drink." He stares at a pile of papers. He does nothing to them but stare. He's stalling. He asked me here but doesn't know what to do with me now that I arrived.

I break the ice. "Thanks for the aspirin and water." My head falls in shame. "I made an ass out of myself, and I'm embarrassed."

"You've got nothing to be embarrassed about, Kat." He grimaces as he says my nickname. "Oh, hell, I hate calling you that name. It's almost painful."

I want to laugh, but this isn't a laughing matter. "It's not my intention to cause you pain."

He looks up with eyes full of despair. I don't know what's going on in his head, but I want to pull him close to me and comfort him.

"I'm in pain every moment I can't have you in my arms. It kills me every night I can't hear your voice," he confesses. "I'm a jealous fool. I can't have you, but I don't want anyone else to have you either. I'm a complete asshole." He grabs the sides of his head and runs both hands through his hair.

"Damon, you can have me. All you need to do is ask. I've been yours since the day I took your arm and you walked me to the limousine. There isn't a minute I don't think about you." I stare into his glacial eyes and see them melt before me. "I sleep with that silk scarf like it can magically make you appear. I haven't put that beautiful dress away, because looking at it makes me feel closer to you."

We stand, and step by step, we close the gap until I'm in front of him with my face pressed against his chest. I can't contain my emotions and tears run down my cheeks.

Strong arms hug me tightly.

"I have no right to you," he says. "I did everything to get you to stay away. I've even been cruel at times."

"Stop. You've mostly been kind and generous and always noble. You took me home Saturday and put me safely to bed. I was in a vulnerable position, and you acted like a gentleman. Your mom would be proud."

"I don't know what I'm doing. I'm on unfamiliar ground, and I don't know how to act."

"Kiss me. Let me in. Let me love you." I reach up and place my palm on his cheek.

He leans into my touch. "I don't know if I can. I want to feel your love, but I don't know where to start."

I pull him to the couch and frame his face with my hands. "We start small and work on this together, one step at a time."

"One kiss at a time." He presses his lips to mine before walking to the door and talking to Greta. When he returns, he resumes kissing me. I don't know how much time passed, but the sun sits low in the sky when we come up for air. My lips are chapped, and my jaw is tired, but I'm happy.

"Can I get you something to drink?" he asks.

I jump up and walk to the bar. "Let *me* get *you* something. What do you want?"

"I want you, but I'll settle for a diet soda."

"Why settle when you can have both?" I pour two diet sodas and walk back to where he sits.

"Come here," he grips my hips and pulls me onto his lap.

I nearly spill the sodas as he buries his face in my hair and draws in a long, deep breath like he may never get another.

When he leans back, I hand him his drink and tease him for keeping me so long. "When I get fired tomorrow, I'm blaming you. I'll have to go to Java Joes and beg them to take me back."

He chuckles. "I know your boss, and I took care of it. Greta called Trevor and told him you were detained and would return tomorrow."

"I'm excused for the day? What should we do?"

"Let's go eat, and then I want to show you my house." He takes my hand and leads me out the door. "Greta, I won't be back until tomorrow. Send all my calls to voicemail."

Greta smiles at both of us. "Have a great night, Mr. Noble, Ms. Cross." Her giggle follows us down the hallway.

Damon guides me into his private elevator that goes directly to the garage. When the door closes, he pins me against the wall, crashing his mouth against mine until I am dizzy with ecstasy.

"Are there security cameras in here?" I ask between kisses.

"There are cameras everywhere, except for my office and the bathrooms. Does it make you nervous?" His hand roams over the curve of my bottom. "Is it exciting to know someone might watch?"

"Is that why you have a glass floor above the VIP lounge? Is it because you're a voyeur?" I look into his eyes, because if he hasn't shuttered his emotions, his eyes never lie. "Is that your thing?"

"No, I'm not a voyeur, although I could spend my life watching you," he sighs. "Saturday night after I undressed you, I wanted to sit on the side of your bed and watch you all night, but my mom raised me to be a better man. As for the glass floor, it was an interesting concept, and I wanted to try it. I wish I could have given you the club tour myself."

"I took the self-guided tour, but I'd love to have a more private experience," I whisper in his ear.

"I can arrange that."

We reach the garage floor and rush to his Mustang. He opens my door and kisses me before I slide into the bucket seat.

"Where's your car?" He looks around for my yellow sedan.

"I park all the way around the corner so you won't see it."

"You could have told me. I wouldn't interfere with your work."

"You already have. I'd rather kiss my Viking god than make phone calls, but I have a project to complete."

He backs out of his spot and exits the garage. "I understand the importance of finding success on your own, and I promise to stay clear as much as possible, but it's the only promise I can make at this time."

Damon drives to Tony's Italian Restaurant, where there's a private table waiting in the corner.

We order two different items from the menu to share.

"Would you like wine?"

I think back to when he told me people who drink make poor decisions. "Heavens no. I don't think I ever want another drink. I should have listened to you, but you frustrated me, and I made a poor choice."

"I guess you can say I already drove you to drink. I'm so sorry." He squeezes my hands and brings them to his lips. "I promise I'll do my best to open up to you. I'll consider your feelings before my own, and I'll try to unlock my heart."

"I can't ask for any more than that." I could, but being here with Damon and him promising to try is more than I imagined possible.

Our food arrives, and we take turns feeding each other bites of both dishes. He has baked ziti, and I have chicken parmigiana. We talk about work and what we're accomplishing.

He likes that I work for him. My proximity gives him access to me all day long. I need to set boundaries, otherwise, I'll never leave his office. But tonight isn't about limitations, it's about possibilities.

"Tell me about your house?" I lean forward on my elbows and wait for him to respond.

"Rather than tell you, I'll show you. Are you ready?"

I'm not sure what he's asking, but I nod because whatever Damon is offering, I'd be a fool to pass up.

He pays the bill, and we're on our way. We drive up a long, winding road and come to a stop in front of a large iron gate.

"What's with the security gates?" Both Damon and his mother have elaborate security systems.

"It's necessary. I have a lot of assets to protect, and there are a lot of not-so-nice people in the world."

He punches in a code, the gate swings open, and we drive a hundred feet into the garage. Next to where he parks sits a beautiful orange and black Charger.

"You have excellent taste in cars. What made you choose them when you could have anything in the world?"

"I love American muscle cars. When I was a kid, I had pictures of Mustangs all over my room. My brother had pictures of Chargers. I bought one of each. The Charger hasn't moved since Roman's death. I'm partial to the Shelby, but I like the Cobra too. I've never been a fan of the Saleen. My first car was a 65 Shelby GT 350. She was beautiful but didn't have the power and amenities of today's models." He pats the steering wheel. "I've had this one for about two years. I trade it in every two years and go back and forth between a convertible and a hardtop. The next one will be a convertible."

With my hand in his, we enter his house in the kitchen. State-of-the-art appliances and designer finishes are everywhere. We move toward the living room where warm colors and plush furniture decorate the masculine interior.

"How big is this place?" Looking at the size of the kitchen and living room, I imagine what the rest is like.

"Roughly five thousand square feet. It has four bedrooms, five bathrooms, a living room, a recreation room, a theater, and a kitchen. There's a formal dining room, although I haven't used it. Perhaps we can break it in together."

"Are you asking me on a date?" I tease.

"As a matter of fact, I am." He nods. "How about dinner and a movie next Friday night?"

"I'd love to go on a date with you."

"I'm looking forward to it myself." Walking to the refrigerator, he pulls two soda cans out and pops them open.

"Was that hard to do?"

He looks at me quizzically. "Was what hard to do?"

"Ask me on a date?"

"Terrifyingly difficult."

I can't tell whether he's serious or joking, but either way, I believe there's some truth to his statement.

"You did well."

"Come out here with me." He points to the french doors. "The view is the reason I bought this house."

I step onto a massive deck overlooking a canyon. The sky packed with stars—something I don't see living in the city, but up here in the hills, the stars twinkle like a million diamonds in the sky.

After setting the sodas down, he stands behind me and pulls my back to his chest. I'm happy to relax and stare into the starry night.

"Thanks for such a wonderful night. There's nowhere I'd rather be than here with you."

"You're so sweet and forgiving. I don't think there's a mean bone in your body. I definitely don't deserve you."

"Emma says the same thing, but she thinks it's because I had a good life and no baggage."

His hug tightens. "I have enough baggage for both of us. You stay sweet, and I'll bear the worries of the world on your behalf."

"How about we share in the burdens? Something tells me you've been carrying them much too long on your own."

I pivot to face him, wrap my arms around his middle, and hang on tight. I know the journey with Damon won't be easy. There are rough roads ahead, but I hope the trip is worth it.

We move to a chaise lounge, and I sit between his legs with my head resting against his chest. I exhale slowly, trying to get a handle on my life. Damon unleashed something in me—something wild and carefree and scary and exciting.

What starts out as a simple kiss turns into so much more. He moves in to kiss me again, and I open my mouth to taste and savor him. It's a lifetime before we come up for air, but when we do, goose bumps spread across my skin. The kiss? The weather?

He wraps himself around me and offers his heat for several minutes, then says, "I should get you home. It's getting late."

"I didn't get the full tour yet," I complain.

He tips my chin to look into my eyes. "I'll give you a comprehensive tour on Friday. Is there a particular movie you want to see?" He helps me up and walks me into the house.

"What's new on video?"

"How about that new movie about the female police officers? It's supposed to be funny." He places our glasses in the sink and moves with me to the garage.

"I don't think it's out yet."

"Doesn't matter. I can get it." He gives me one of those looks that says I shouldn't doubt him.

"Really?" I look at him, surprised. "I'd love to see it."

"Done. I promise you a night to remember. Now, let's get you home?"

I push my lower lip out in a pout. "If I must."

"Behave, and I might tuck you in." He nips at my protruding lip.

"Okay." I smile. "And if *you're* good, I'll let you undress me again."

"You're killing me," he says.

"Join my club."

We hold hands all the way to my house, where we find Emma and Anthony tucked next to each watching a scary movie.

"Hi, guys." I pull Damon behind me to my room. "Bye, guys." I stop for nothing because I don't want him to get sidetracked or change his mind about tucking me in.

"You guys keep it down in there!" Em yells.

Damon stands still in the center of my room, focused on my queen-sized bed.

"I should go," he says.

"You promised you'd tuck me in, and I have no intention of letting you off the hook."

"Are you really going to torture me?" His eyes plead with mine.

"You undressed me, but I wasn't sober enough to enjoy the experience. I demand a do-over." What will it feel like to have this man remove my clothes?

He picks me up like I'm a featherweight and tosses me on the bed. He creeps up to cover me with his body—his weight on me is divine.

I run my hands through his hair, dragging my fingers softly down to the sensitive area above his collarbone. Rising up, I run my tongue over his pulsing artery and feel his heart race with mine.

"Who do you think I am, woman? I don't have superpowers."

He straddles my body while he unbuttons my dress. The slowness of his movements tortures me. One button, then a kiss. Another button and a kiss. The pattern repeats until the buttons are undone, and the front of my dress lies open to my waist.

He stares at me like an artist looks at a canvas, then lifts my dress free of my hips. Once it's hoisted over my head, I'm left wearing only my bra and underwear.

If I had known he'd undress me tonight, I'd have chosen sexier lingerie.

He moves above me. The clear outline of his arousal takes my breath away.

A cocky grin softens his expression.

"You're so damn beautiful." His hands slide up my sides while his lips move against mine. Sometime between the beginning and the end of the kiss, my bra disappears.

He cups my breasts as if testing their weight and size. "Look at you lying here so sexy."

His eyes take in every part of me while his hands knead my aching breasts.

I close my eyes to enjoy the miracle of the moment. "That's so nice." My hum floats through the air.

"I need to go home before you regret tonight," he blurts out.

I grab hold of him before he can bolt. "There's nothing about tonight that I'll regret."

"I want our first time to be perfect. I owe you the fairytale experience."

He rolls to his side and pulls me into the curve of his body, then tugs the covers over us, and we relax into each other.

CHAPTER THIRTEEN

The alarm goes off at six o'clock, and when I roll over, I run smack dab into a solid wall of muscle. Damon reaches for my phone and beats at it until the relentless chirping stops.

My hand rests on his chest while his arm cradles me. His free hand caresses my arm to brush the side of my breast. "More of that," I beg.

"We need to get up, or we'll never leave this room. Five more minutes of this, and I won't be able to let you go."

"You drive a hard bargain, and I would prefer to stay, but I can't. You already made me miss work yesterday, and now I have to work harder today to catch up."

"I'll drop you off before I go home and shower. Can you join me for lunch around noon?"

"I'd love to have lunch with you. Are we still going to have our book club meeting on Wednesday?" I ask with a hopeful gaze. "It's a long time until our Friday date."

"Wednesday is on, but you have to find time to read the next fifty pages. It's my turn to choose the restaurant and my turn to buy."

"I'm an overachiever. I'll get it done."

I jump up, wearing nothing but my underwear, and make a beeline for the bathroom. When I emerge from my shower, Damon is nowhere in sight. I'm in the living room putting on my shoes when he walks through the front door with two coffee cups and a bag of pastries.

"Are you wooing me, Mr. Noble? Pastries and coffee are a sure-fire way to my heart."

"You better look at what I brought before you offer your heart."

"Good advice. What did you bring?"

"I brought a croissant, a chocolate donut, an apple fritter, and a banana muffin."

"For this selection, you get my hugs and kisses, but if there was a cheese Danish, I'd give you my soul."

"Pay up, then. I believe you owe me hugs and kisses."

He pulls me into his arms, and his lips caress mine. It's a good thing he's holding me because his touch makes me unsteady.

"Get a room," Em says when Anthony and her walk into the living room.

I'm in no hurry to leave Damon's embrace, so I ignore her while we draw our kiss to a close.

"Gotta run, Em. I don't want to be late to the office." I pick up my purse and give her a hug.

"I'll be home after work," Em says. "You've got some splainen to do."

"A girl never tells her secrets." I grab the coffee, pastries, and Damon's hand, and we're off.

He drops me off at the front of the building and speeds away. I make it to my cubicle to find the phone's red light blinking like a beacon. I press in my retrieval code and listen to the messages that have accumulated since my absence yesterday afternoon.

I wish they were all positive, but they aren't. I wanted to make sure Anthony Haywood's was represented in the gift bags and thought gift cards for nice cutlery or kitchen gadgets would be a nice tie-in. Unfortunately, the knife company doesn't want to take part.

The one hundred cookbooks I got will help, and the leading manufacturer of stand mixers agreed to donate gift certificates for each bag. They'll ship them to each of our VIP guests. Pleased with the way things are turning out, I lean back in my chair and smile.

"Hey, Kat. Glad you could join us." Trevor leans over my shoulder, looking at the list of my latest acquisitions. "Nice job."

"I'm happy with my progress. I beat your estimate, and I'm determined to achieve my goal of getting them to be worth ten thousand."

"Tell me how you ended up helping Mr. Noble yesterday. I never had an intern called up for a project before, and I've been here a long time." He eyes me with suspicion.

I want to be honest, but I want to protect Damon's privacy, so I skate the issue the best I can.

"I know him outside of work. I didn't tell him I'd applied for the internship, because I didn't want him to interfere. When he saw me walking out of the elevator yesterday, it surprised him, and he asked me to go to his office to explain. I'm sorry it interfered with my work; it won't happen again."

"Kat, when the president's secretary calls and tells you Mr. Noble is detaining one of your interns, you don't ask questions." Trevor gets close enough for secrets. "Since you know him, maybe you can tell me if he's..." He stalls for a minute before blurting, "Does he like men or women?"

I stare at Trevor like he'd grown a third eye. Is he asking because he's interested in Damon or fishing for gossip? Feeling protective, I don't want a scandal surrounding his sexuality.

"He's not gay, Trevor." My blush gives me away, but I'll be damned if anyone spreads rumors about Damon.

"Darn. He's a fine-looking man. I thought for sure there was a chance ... he dresses too nice to be straight."

"I can assure you Damon's heterosexual, and he dresses nicely because he has impeccable style and taste."

"You can assure me, huh? Tell me ... is Mr. Noble a good kisser? Maybe I should say *Damon* since you're on a cozy, first-name basis with him."

"I'm a friend of the family and attend charity events with him and his mother. Stop prying for information. I'm not your go-to source for gossip." I tap my chin. "I'm assuming your preference is for men similar to Damon?"

"I prefer them to know they're gay, but if you think I can persuade Mr. Noble to try the other side, I might enjoy the challenge."

"Give it up. It will never happen."

Trevor staggers backward with his forearm against his head as if he may faint. "I'm crestfallen."

"Don't you have anything else to do besides bother me?"

"Yes, but it's so much fun to watch you blush." He squeezes my shoulder before he leaves.

I spend the next three hours organizing deliveries and getting donations. At exactly twelve o'clock, I turn off my computer and make my way to Damon's office.

"Good afternoon, Ms. Cross."

"Hello, Greta. It's so nice to see you today. How are you?"

"Excellent, Ms. Cross. How about you?"

"Marvelous. Is Mr. Noble in?"

"Go on in. He's waiting for you. Enjoy your lunch."

I enter his private office without so much as an announcement. I wanted him today, and I wondered how a person can crave someone after just four hours.

Closing the door behind me, I glance around the large office and find him by the window setting the table for our lunch. He's in deep thought as he places the silverware in their proper places and pours us a soda.

I lean against the door and stare at him. When he sees me, he enchants me with his smile. I want this man so much.

"What are you doing over there? This is where all the action is," he says.

"Really? What kind of action are you offering?"

"What I have in mind will take more than an hour, so you'll have to settle for a quick lunch. I ordered soup and salad. Eating heavy makes me feel sleepy, and then I'm less productive."

I sit at the table and place the napkin in my lap. I didn't approach him for a kiss or a hug but hope he'll give me one on his own accord. Sleeping with him last night was a major step, and I don't want to push him too far—too fast.

"I bet you're fabulous when you're at the top of your game."

"Are you being naughty again? If you finished your reading for the week, you'd know what happens to naughty girls."

"I'm intrigued. I'll rush home after work and read the next installment." He's so put together in his custom gray suit, crisp white shirt, and red tie. "I see you made it home and back in time."

"I did. Kat, last night was good—really good."

"Did you know that I've never spent the night in a man's arms? I'm glad you were my first."

A dark look clouds his expression. It's not a look of passion, but a look of distrust. "Your first? Do you plan to have others?" His voice challenges me.

"All I meant was you're the first man to spend the night. I didn't mean to imply I was looking for others." Whoever she was, did a number on him.

"I'm sorry I misinterpreted your response and overreacted."

"You seem to do that a lot."

"You are right, and I'm sorry. These are my burdens to bear."

"You don't have to bear them by yourself."

He reaches out to cover my hand, and I'm sure he is going to open up.

"Let's leave it for now." And the subject is closed.

"Are you having a good day?"

"The beginning was so great. Everything since then has been a disappointment until now, but things are looking up." He nods to the couch. "Do you want to sit with me for a few minutes?"

"Sure. I don't have to be back until one." Sitting on the couch can only mean more kisses, and if I can't get information from Damon, then I'll settle for what I can get. I'm not one that gives up easily. One day he'll let me in.

"How many pastries did you eat this morning?" he asks.

"I ate two. Why?"

"You're still in my debt because I only received compensation for one. We haven't even discussed the price for the coffee or the ride."

"Those sound like expensive pastries, Mr. Noble. I'm not sure I can afford you."

"We can draw up an installment plan." He lifts his broad shoulders. "I'll charge you interest, and I should warn you, my rates are high."

"Hmm ... I'll make a down payment now, but before I leave, add my bill, so I know what I owe you." I smirk.

"We could arrange scheduled payments. I'd be happy to draw up the agreement."

"You're a shrewd businessman." I love it when playful Damon is present because he's so much fun.

He scoops me up and sits me on his lap, where he plays with my hair and nibbles on my lip. His hand comes up to cradle my cheek while his thumb brushes lightly over the highest part of my cheekbone.

"Your blue eyes, combined with your blonde hair, remind me of an angel. All you need is a halo."

"I'm no angel," I say.

"You're my angel."

This man muddles my brain, first with his kisses and now with his words.

"I'm happy to be yours."

"What does your schedule look like this week?" His thumb slides down my cheek until he is softly caressing my lower lip. He stares at me like a lion stalking his prey.

"I have to study tonight and read several pages for my book club meeting tomorrow night. I have lunch free all week, and Thursday night isn't booked yet. Friday night, I have a date with this sizzling, Viking god."

The clock on his desk ticks closer to one o'clock and our time is almost up.

He skims his lips across mine. "I'll call you later, okay?"

"I look forward to it." After a deeper kiss, I unwrap myself from his tight embrace and say goodbye. Then I leave his office and go to the third floor to finish my shift.

CHAPTER FOURTEEN

"I want every dirty detail." Em pulls me inside and forces me to sit on the couch by pressing my shoulders down.

"There isn't much to tell," I say. "Damon found out I worked in the building, and that led to a meeting in his office. We shared some amazing kisses that led to dinner. He took me to his house, we kissed more, and he drove me home. That's all there is to report."

"Bullshit. He spent the night, and I walked out of my room to find you both nearly stripping each other naked in the living room." Em crosses her arms in front of her and narrows her eyes. She tries to bully me into giving her more, but there isn't anything else to share.

"We slept, Em. The plan was for him to tuck me in and leave, but he didn't. When I went to the Philharmonic with him and his mother, I got angry with him for ignoring me. I had way too much to drink, and he ended up bringing me home, undressing me, and putting me to bed."

"What? Did he do anything inappropriate?" She sounds indignant and angry. The one thing I can count on is Em having my back.

"No, he behaved, but he saw parts of me when he changed me, and I insisted on a do-over. Last night was it."

"Go on," she prompts.

"Em, there isn't anything else to tell. We kissed, and he undressed me, then he spooned me, and we fell asleep. We didn't have sex, although he wouldn't have had to beg me because I more than want him." I'm a twenty-three-year-old woman with two lovers and three experiences to my name. I want to end this dry spell and find out what all the hubbub is about.

"Tell me if I have this correct. You were naked in his arms all night, and he didn't even try to have sex with you?" She shakes her head. "Something is wrong with that man. I don't know any guy who can lie next to a willing woman and not want to ... you know."

"It's not like he didn't want to. He was totally aroused, but he didn't want it to be like that. He said something about making our first time perfect. He considered me, and that felt good. Why didn't you tell me how nice it is to sleep with a man?"

"It is nice, isn't it?" She stares across the room with a dreamy look in her eyes, no doubt reliving a moment in her mind, and I bet it has something to do with Anthony.

"How are things with Mr. Haywood?"

"Oh, you know, the same old earth-shattering sex, titillating conversation, great food. Same stuff, different day." She grins at me, then laughs. "It's amazing. Where was this man my whole life?"

"Maybe the timing wasn't right, and now it is." I'm a true believer that things happen for a reason.

"Hmm, maybe." She snaps out of wherever her head was. "Damon better treat you well, because if he doesn't, I'll hunt him down and hurt him."

"He's a good man, but he's complicated. His brother died when Damon was twenty, and everything seems to stem from that tragic event. There's so much I don't know."

"He's not a puppy for you to rescue."

"I'm not a puppy rescuer."

"No, you're right. You're a people rescuer, and it looks like he's your next project."

"He's not a project, but it would be nice to know what happened to him."

"Have you considered asking him?"

"I'm not going to ask him. He'll tell me on his own when he's ready."

"You're patient and kind. I remember the little girl who held me night after night while I cried in her arms." She looks sad at the memory. "I wouldn't have made it through the death of my mother without you. You've always been an old soul, but I often wonder if you're getting what you need from the people around you."

"If I can get him naked and in bed, then I'll be closer to getting what I need. We're staying at his house this weekend. He has a theater, and somehow, he's able to get a new release."

"It goes back to, 'it's not what you know, but who you know,' and Damon knows powerful people."

"Do you have any advice for me? How am I supposed to seduce this man when he could have anyone in the world?"

"Look at you. You're gorgeous, and what makes you even more beautiful is you're not aware of how alluring you are. Men fall all over themselves when you're around."

"That is so not true, and you know it. Men steer clear of me."

"No, they don't. It's that innocence that draws them in."

"Em, I'm not innocent. I've experienced things."

"Kat, do you really think banging that boy in the back seat was an authentic sexual experience? What was he, eighteen? He had no idea what he was doing. What guy takes his girlfriend out to a field and does it in the back seat? He could have at least laid out a blanket on the ground, but he was an idiot. You need someone to treat you right; someone who doesn't want to have sex but wants to make love. I hope Damon is that guy."

"Me too."

"Damaged men can be difficult. Be careful, Kat."

"Thanks, Em. I missed you, and I'm so glad you're happy. It's been a long time coming."

She reaches up to hug me. "I love you." She squeezes me tight before leaning back. "If Friday is the big night, we need to get you ready. Do you have birth control?"

"Yes, Mom." I roll my eyes. "I started the shots last year when I thought things would go in that direction with Tommy. I get them regularly because I almost never have a period anymore, and I like that."

"Until you know his sexual past, the rule is no glove, no love. Use condoms. I don't want you getting an STI from him."

"Good advice. What else do I need to know?"

"Make sure he satisfies your needs before his own. There's nothing worse than a selfish lover. I'm not saying you have to keep tabs. It's rarely a one-for-one deal, but it's no fun if you're the only one giving."

"Got it."

"Do you have a good waxer?"

"What?" I shoot her a look of disbelief. "What do I need a waxer for?"

"You want to keep yourself groomed. No one wants to make love to Sasquatch. Get it waxed or trim it up. I wax, but some people feel weird about having no hair."

"I'll trim."

"Fine. What will you wear?"

"A dress? Whatever I wear to work is what I'll wear to his house."

"Nope. Bring a change of clothes so you'll be fresh. In fact, let's go shopping Thursday when you get home. A new outfit will boost your confidence."

"I like clothes as much as I like food. Let's get dinner too."

Once the plans are made, I spend the rest of my night doing

homework. I have three tests this week and haven't devoted much time to studying. Damon and work are a distraction.

After three hours of writing and test prep, I pick up *Bound* and climb into bed.

The agreement between the characters heads in a kinky direction with him being the dominant and her the submissive. I finish the fifty pages, close the book, and ponder their situation. How much would I put up with to be with the person I want? Is it true there is a fine line between pain and pleasure? Can pain become pleasure? It's an interesting question.

CHAPTER FIFTEEN

My leather bags arrive, and I'm excited to fill them.

Trevor gets me a large, empty room with several tables to assemble the gift bags. I line one row with the bags and use the other tables to organize the donations.

At noon, I race upstairs to collect my kisses.

Lunch has become my guilty pleasure. I get an uninterrupted hour with Damon, and we get to snuggle and kiss.

"I hear the gift bags you're assembling are incredible. How did you get so many companies to donate in this economy?"

"I've been taking charm lessons from Damon Noble. He's really talented. I'm sure he could charm the pants off anyone."

"I only want to charm the pants off you. What do you think the chances are of me getting you out of your pants this weekend?" He rubs my thigh; the heat from his touch burns my skin.

"If I were a betting girl, I'd say the odds are in your favor. I may not have a lot of experience, but I want you, and I'm willing to be the student if you will teach me."

He places his chin between his thumb and his index finger and looks at me through hooded eyes.

"This might be an awkward question, but just how much experience do you have? I only ask because it will influence how we approach our first time together."

"I'm not embarrassed by the question. I always try to remain open and honest about my life." I fumble with the hem of my shirt. "I'm not a virgin, but my experiences can't be described as extensive either. Unfortunately, it was like waiting for fireworks and finding out I got a dud."

"I'll do my best to show you fireworks," he whispers with his warm breath grazing my neck.

A chill runs down my spine. "I know you can ignite a fire in me, but with these lunches and your kisses, I'm liable to burn up before Friday."

"Go back to work, and I'll pick you up at seven for book club and dinner."

He swats my behind as I walk toward the door.

I PACE the living room floor waiting for Damon to arrive. After our touchy-feely lunch, I'm full of tension and can't sit still. When I see his Mustang pull around the corner, I am in the car before it rolls to a complete stop.

"I would have gotten out and opened the door for you, Angel."

"I know, but I'm eager to see you." Once I'm in his car, I lean toward him and pucker my lips.

His press firmly against mine, causing my heart to skip a beat.

"Now I'm Angel?" He hates calling me Kat, but as long as he chooses the nickname, then it's okay?

"It fits you." He touches my cheek. "Angelic face, cupid lips, saintly eyes, and hair that shines like a halo."

"It's sweet. No one has ever called me anything other than Kat."

I hear him grumble at the mention of my nickname. "What's so bad about the name Kat?"

"We've talked about this before. I guess I'm a traditionalist and like to call people by their given names. However, since everyone around you insists on calling you by a nickname, I at least gave you one that fits."

"Fair enough. I'm happy to be your angel." I buckle in. "Where are we eating?"

"A quiet little steakhouse in Manhattan Beach, and then we'll take a stroll along the shore." I hold his hand until we arrive at the restaurant.

Tucked into a corner booth in the back, he scoots in close to me, so our thighs are touching, and his hand sits on my bare knee.

Damon orders for both of us, which I like because there is something sexy about confidence—about a man who seems like he could rule the world.

"What are you thinking about?" he asks as his hand gently runs up my thigh.

"I can't think about much of anything with you caressing me. But I am hoping that on Friday night, you might put out the fire you ignited this afternoon."

He looks at me in amazement. "I've never been with a girl who just says what's on her mind. I like that about you."

I'd like that about you too if you shared.

Instead of saying what I really think for fear it will cause an argument, I go with something else. "I aim to please," I beam. "Tell me ... did you enjoy the last fifty pages of the book?"

The waiter delivers two plates, both with sea bass and rice pilaf. Off to the side are grilled asparagus spears. We continue to talk as we enjoy our dinner.

"What's not to like?" he asks. "He told her what he likes, and she's willing to try it. That seems diplomatic."

"There's nothing democratic about their relationship. I couldn't relinquish that much power to a man."

"You just answered the question from last week. I asked how far you'd go for the person you cared about."

"I wouldn't go far enough to lose myself in the process, but I'm willing to negotiate like she did. I say what's on my mind, and that isn't a good trait for a submissive. My bottom would be sore all the time from the spankings I'd get for misbehaving."

"Does that turn you on or off?" He lifts his brow.

"I've given that some thought and researched the subject. Apparently, there's some kind of pain-pleasure connection. It has something to do with the sting, the heat from the contact, and the vibration it creates. Anticipation is also a big component. I don't have a desire to be spanked, so I wouldn't consider it a turn-on, but it doesn't send me running for the hills either. I'd be willing to consider it as long as it was under the right conditions."

"Thank goodness that's not my thing. I'd never spank you. A swat on your backend while you're walking by, maybe, but nothing more. There are other ways to excite you, other ways to make you tingle, other ways to warm your skin."

"You have me in a state as it is."

He chuckles. "You would be a bad poker player. All your cards are out for me to see. I haven't even played my hand, and you're folding yours."

"What's a girl supposed to do?" I ask. "You kiss me in a way that sets my panties aflame, and then you pull back, only to ignite everything again. Just when I think I'm catching my breath, you run your hand up to my nether regions and make me lose myself once more. I can't take much more of this."

"It hasn't been easy for me either. Just looking at you makes me hard." His head lowers, and I follow his gaze to his growing length.

"Good. I'm glad you're suffering too."

"I can relieve that torment. All you have to do is sit back and relax, and I'll take that ache away," he whispers in my ear.

"What are you talking about?" He rubs my thigh and lets his fingers trail up the inside of my leg.

He barely touches me, and my body quivers.

"Let me show you. No one will see." His tongue lightly flicks my earlobe, sending prickles of awareness throughout my body.

Oh, my God, what's he talking about? We're in a restaurant, in the company of other diners.

"We're in a public place, where people can see us." I hiss under my breath.

"You asked me what my thing was a while back, and honestly, I like the excitement of it all."

Have I lost my mind? I'm in a restaurant booth with a man who obviously has his own kind of kink going on, and he wants to pleasure me right here, right now. What's crazy is, I'm considering it.

How far would I go for someone I care about?

I lean into him, and he whispers, "Relax and enjoy, Angel."

With his hand between my legs and his fingers working my body, I do exactly what he says. I lean back and enjoy. The things he does to me sends me over the edge in seconds flat.

I catch my breath and see his cocky smile.

He's not the only one who can play naughty games. I want to straddle this man right now, but everyone would notice, so I reciprocate in kind.

"Now it's your turn to just lie back and relax," I tell him.

With several strokes of my hand, Damon Noble submits to me.

I tuck the soiled napkin into my purse, feeling victorious.

"Can I offer you dessert?" the waiter asks when he returns.

Damon and I burst into laughter. I respond to the waiter's question because Damon can't control himself.

"No, thank you. We've already indulged, but we'd like decaf coffee. One with cream, please."

The waiter walks away as Damon continues to chuckle. Within minutes, the waiter is back with our coffee, and we sit and talk.

"Do you feel better now?" he asks.

"I've never done anything so brazen. It scared me, but it was mind-blowing. What if someone had caught us?"

"The trick is to act as naturally as you can. Don't make a lot of noise and keep your body movements to a minimum—or at least concealed by the table. You tucked your face into my chest and buried your moans against my shirt. No one was the wiser. The excitement comes from the possibility of getting caught. You did well."

"So, this is your thing? You like to have sex in public places?"

I ask for clarification because I'm not sure how I feel about the whole experience Did I like it? Would I do it again? I'm not sure.

"I wouldn't say it's my *thing*, but I do like the thrill of it. I particularly enjoyed pleasing you. Taking care of me came as a pleasant surprise."

I remember Em's advice and say, "I'm not a lazy lover."

"I can see that."

Damon pays the bill, and we stroll onto the beach, listening to the waves and sitting near the water to watch them break.

My eyes find his. "Can I ask you a personal question? I wouldn't pry, but since we've moved to a sexual relationship, I need the answers."

He looks at me for a minute. "You can ask, and I'll do my best to answer."

At least he's honest. I can't expect him to lay his entire life out in front of me after one date—one orgasm.

"I know you don't date, but you must relieve your sexual tension somehow. A man like you doesn't seem like he'd be the celibate type. How do you satisfy your needs?"

Even in the moonlight, I see a blush rise to his cheeks, and it's cute.

"I never wanted to get involved in another relationship, so I hired escorts for business, and I hired others for sex. If I didn't do that, I took care of myself."

"You use prostitutes?" My jaw drops open.

"I suppose you could think of it that way, but to me, it's no-strings-attached sex. I don't drive down to Sunset Boulevard and pull over to ask the corner hooker if she's free. There are services for sex. You can buy just about anything you want if you have enough money." He stares out at the sea. "The girls I hire are professionals: they take care of themselves by taking care of me. Does it bother you?"

"Are you still using their services?" It's not like we have an exclusive relationship, but I want to know what I'm getting myself into, and if he's using hookers, I'm out.

"The minute I met you, I stopped seeing the others."

Something warm settles in my heart. "Then it doesn't bother me."

He looks relieved—almost happy. With my hand in his, he helps me to my feet and kisses the air from my lungs.

"I'll never cheat on you, Katarina. I'm a one-woman man, and I expect the same from you. I haven't had good experiences in the past, so it's difficult for me to trust."

"I'm not a cheater either. Infidelity is a deal breaker."

"One kiss at a time, then?" he asks.

"One kiss at a time."

"Shall I take you home? It's getting late."

I'm disappointed the date is ending, but we have work tomorrow. "Do you want to stay the night?"

"I wish I could, but I have an early morning meeting. We can meet for lunch again if that works for you."

"Will you kiss me?"

"Is that all you want?"

I want it all, but I'm afraid to tell him.

CHAPTER SIXTEEN

I find a dozen red roses interspersed with baby's breath on my desk. The card attached to the plastic pick says, "Angel" on the envelope.

Dinner last night was the most amazing and moving experience of my life.

With Affection,

Damon.

A giggle bubbles up from inside me. He signed the card, "With Affection." That has to mean something.

"Ooh, flowers! Who are they from?" Trevor is like a ninja; I never hear him approach until he's beside me.

"It's none of your business. Don't you have something better to do than skulk around my desk?" I feel comfortable teasing Trevor because he dishes out more than he gets.

We work closely together, and I've become fond of him. I'd even call him my friend.

Trevor laughs. "I'm like a sprite. I don't walk—I float. It's a fabulous skill to have when you want to know the inside scoop on something. No one hears you coming." He reaches for the card in my hand, but I'm quicker and move it out of his reach. "I bet it's from your lover boy upstairs."

"He's not my lover boy. Besides, why would he send me flowers?"

"I can read you like a book because your face doesn't allow you to lie." He inhales the scent of a rose and steps back. "An entire box of books arrived for you this morning. I put them in the assembly room."

The box of books he is referring to is *Bound*. I thought it would be fun to tie all the books with red scarves and place them in the top of the bag. It's an unspoken message to Damon and a little fun for the guests.

"I'm almost finished with the gift bags. What do you want me to help with after that?" The more I learn, the more I can sell myself to my future employer.

"I need help keeping our headliner happy. Can you make sure the dressing rooms are stocked with everything they need?"

"Do I finally get to know who the band is? I thought that was a secret."

"You've earned my trust. If you won't divulge anything about your relationship with Damon, then I figure I can tell you Reluctant Capitalists is playing for the grand opening."

I suck in a breath. "You're kidding? You don't have the actual band playing on opening night. It's a cover band, right?"

"They're the real deal, and I've heard they're picky." He leans against the desk. "They like certain liquor, flowers, and foods. I'll tell you what I know, but you need to dig deeper. Happy bands mean great shows. The opening experience can make or break a club, so there's a lot riding on this."

"If you get me their manager's name, I'll get on it right away."

He picks up a sticky note and writes something down. "I'll make sure you have everything I have."

"Perfect, and I'll make sure they're the happiest band ever."

"Seriously, though, Kat, they better be."

Trevor calling me Kat made me think of how Damon only calls me Katarina, and I love the way it sounds, in fact, I think I prefer it.

"Hey Trevor, can you call me by my full name? I am kind of partial to the sound."

"No problem, *Katarina*. Now, go finish the bags, girl, so you can earn your keep," he jokes.

"You're a hard taskmaster." I shoo him away.

"Tell that to my boss, and he can punish me." Trevor bends over and slaps his own ass. I walk past him and smack him myself. He has no idea how close he is to actually knowing things about Damon.

"Mr. Noble isn't your type." I pinch my chin and look him over. "I see you with a gay version of Ryan Gosling."

"Oh, yeah, I'll do Gosling. I'd also like a piece of Ian Somerhalder."

Who wouldn't? "They're both straight, but it's not a bad idea to set your standards high." I wave over my shoulder and head to the assembly room. "I'll see you after lunch."

EVERYTHING I NEED IS HERE, and the only money I spent was on tissue paper, ribbons, and bows—and the one hundred copies of *Bound* that cost fifteen hundred dollars out of my budget.

The retail value is nearly nine thousand dollars per bag. I didn't hit my goal of ten grand, but I'm proud of my accomplishments.

These gift bags have everything from designer chocolates to designer watches. They also include music, movies, books, spa packages, kitchen gadgets, and gourmet foods. A piece of all the elements of Ahz is included, and I would love to receive swag like this.

Why is it the people who can afford everything get stuff for free, and the people who would appreciate it most, never have an opportunity to receive it?

As I tie the last red scarf around the final book, my stomach grumbles, which means it's time to eat—time to see Damon.

"GOOD AFTERNOON, Ms. Cross. Go right in. Mr. Noble is expecting you."

"Thanks, Greta."

Damon sits behind his desk, talking on the phone. I enter quietly, not wanting to disturb him. With a push of a button, the lock clicks behind me, and I stroll to his seat. He smiles and pulls me into his lap without a break in his conversation.

The nearness of his body and the smell of his cologne creates an internal frenzy. I skim my fingers over his chest and follow the path of his buttons down to his belt.

His expression is stern as if warning me to stop, but I feel fearless, and there's no way I'll obey. If he wants obedience, he chose the wrong woman.

Let's see if I can shock Mr. Noble with something unexpected today. Maybe it's time I become a risk-taker.

I spent too many years waiting for some man to give me what I want, but last night, he opened a door I can't close. I can have what I want as long as I go after it.

I ignore his stern look and slide down his body to my knees.

The surprised look on his face is worth the carpet burn I'll get.

My hands run up his thighs, slowly hovering, taunting, teasing.

The hitch of his breath makes me bold. He's having difficulty concentrating.

Bold Kat surfaces, and I unbuckle his belt, unzip his pants, and release him. He springs free as if it had been held hostage for an eternity.

His head falls back, and his eyes close. I know that feeling. It's complete surrender to all the feels.

He strains to contain himself but stays on the phone. Hopefully, this is the most memorable call of his life.

His free hand threads through my hair and guides my head in the rhythm of his choosing, but I'm in charge, and I make the rules. I take control and nip and nibble and suck and lick.

"Max, I'll call you back. Something's come up I need to address immediately."

And just like that, Damon is off the phone.

"What are you doing to me? I can't work with your lips around me. I can't concentrate with you on your knees. You're killing me."

I pause and watch his expression change to pure bliss when I refuse to stop, and he finds his release.

After a few breaths, he lifts me onto his lap. I lay my head on his shoulder and place my hand over his heart. It pounds against his chest only evening out several minutes later.

"Are you sure my competition didn't send you to screw up my negotiations?"

"If they sent someone, they would have sent a professional. I'm an overzealous novice."

"I love a girl who's motivated. That might be the best experience I've had."

"I can now honestly say I've tasted what others have enjoyed."

He gives me a strange look, and when I think about what I said, I realize he thinks I'm referring to others who have tasted him.

"I meant, I'm glad I tried that. I liked it, and I'd do it again."

He stands with me in his arms and carries me to the couch. When he sets me down, he devours my mouth like it was his last meal. He pulls away and looks at me.

"You're sexy lying here on my couch." Something animalistic takes over, and he changes from man to predator.

"I will unleash a storm in you that you can never control."

His lips trail down my chest to kiss me where I've never been kissed before.

The storm he spoke of erupts within me. It's a tsunami or possibly a category five hurricane. Damon is the tide that takes me away and carries me under.

We're both half-dressed, and he's fully aroused. When my eyes latch on to his length, he shakes his head and puts himself together.

"The first time will be meaningful. On my couch is not where I want that to happen." He picks up my underwear and tucks them into his pocket. "I'm keeping these. Finish your day without them for being naughty. The thought of you running around my building without panties is a bigger punishment for me than you."

"Are you serious?"

He ignores the question. "Can we meet for dinner tonight?"

"I can't." My stomach sinks with the weight of disappointment. "I promised to spend time with Em. What about lunch tomorrow?"

He hangs his head. "That won't work. I've got a board meeting that will last most of the afternoon."

"Tomorrow night, then. Should I meet you at your place, or do you have something else in mind?"

He doesn't look like a man who's had enough of me. His eyes are heavy and filled with desire.

"Yes, you can come straight to my place, and I'll take care of everything. You just show up and bring at least one change of clothes—no pajamas because you won't need them. I promise to make sure you won't get cold. Do you remember how to get to my house?"

"Yep, shall I bring wine or something to eat?"

"Just bring yourself. The code to the gate is 0615. Come at six o'clock."

Since Damon and I spent most of my lunch break pleasuring each other, I have a mere ten minutes to gobble up the Caesar salad he ordered.

As I leave the office, the cool air circulates around me, making me fully aware that my panties are in his pocket.

"Have a nice afternoon, Ms. Cross." Every day I see Greta her smile gets bigger. She has to know what's going on between us because she's right outside the door, for goodness sake.

CHAPTER SEVENTEEN

Em and I go to a spa called The Four Elements, where we enjoy a hot stone massage, a body scrub, a manicure, and a pedicure, courtesy of Anthony Haywood.

Every muscle I've tensed up over the last few days relaxes under the masseuse's capable hands. The release today, combined with the spa treatment, turns me to jelly. All I need is a glass of wine, and the world will be perfect.

After our treatments, we arrive at Anthony Haywood's Restaurant. It's standing room only, but there's a table reserved for us. Em offers to go somewhere else, but I don't mind coming here.

She abandons me briefly to say hello to her man, and I take a moment to text Damon and tell him how wonderful the afternoon was.

He responds immediately, letting me know I rocked his world.

When Em comes back, she looks like a teenager in love.

"Anthony made us something special and is delivering it himself."

We sip glasses of merlot and talk about all the things we haven't had time to tell each other. For me, it's the gift bags and how proud I am of how they turned out. Then there's our upcoming graduation, which is only ten days away.

Next week the craziness begins. I have two papers due and two finals to take. Em has one paper and two exams.

She shares her plans to help Anthony with his marketing since it's her major, and I'm pleased to see he values her as a woman, a professional, and a person.

Anthony arrives with two plates, both beautifully presented with lamb chops, rosemary potatoes, and steamed spinach. Everything Em loves. They say the way to a man's heart is through his stomach, but it's the same for Emma.

Before he leaves, Anthony kisses my best friend like he owns her heart, and I'm certain he does. Em and I have been best friends since the seventh grade, and she's never acted so enamored.

"Tomorrow is the big night," Em singsongs.

I blush and look away so she won't read anything into the grin on my face, but when I face her, it's obvious she's on to me.

"Spill it, Cross. Something's happened between you two. Did you give in and put out last night?"

"No, it's not like that. We want it to be life-altering, but we were both too worked up to last until Friday, so we did some other stuff."

She leans in. "I want to know all the dirty details."

"I don't kiss and tell, but I'll say it was amazing."

"Look at you! My virginal friend finally succumbs to the earth-shattering effects of 'other stuff.'"

"I'm not a virgin," I insist much too loudly, but instead of feeling horrified, I laugh.

"There's nothing better than great sex … unless it's great sex with an amazing man. I want you to have it all, girlfriend. Let's toast," she says.

We both raise our wine glasses, and Em proposes a toast.

"Here's to men who will care for and adore us until our dying breaths." We tap our glasses in the obligatory fashion and toss back the rest of our wine.

There's no more time for dining when there's shopping to do.

Em drags me to several stores, where she advises me on lingerie purchases and helps pick out a rocking-hot outfit for tomorrow night.

Our last stop is the drugstore where she equips me with a large box of condoms, new razors for a clean, close shave, and the body butter she swears by.

Back at home, she says, "I love you, and I want this to be the best time of your life. But … if he does anything to hurt you, I'll inflict so much pain on him, he will wish he was never born."

"Easy killer, he is a good man, and I don't see him hurting me intentionally."

"You are right. Besides, all you need to do is rock his word, and he won't know what hit him."

Damon did say I rocked his world and that gave me confidence to be reckless. "I already did that."

Em looks up and shakes her head. "Will you be back by Sunday?"

"That or Monday. I don't have school on Monday, but I have work, so we'll see. I'll text you over the weekend when I come up for air."

"You may never come up for air. Damon doesn't seem like the breathing type." She winks and leaves for her room.

I pack for the weekend before I climb into bed. Like every night before, I check my phone before turning out the lights and find a message from Damon.

Bring the red scarf.
Yours,
Damon

Holy smokes, he wants the scarf. I jump up, grab it, and shove it into my bag. The thought of him and that scarf sends heat through my veins. Groaning, I fluff my pillow and throw myself into it. A long and sleepless night awaits.

CHAPTER EIGHTEEN

I find another dozen roses and a lunchbox waiting on my desk. The card on the flowers only says, "Beautiful" on it.

The lunchbox stumps me. I open it and find a sandwich, chips, an apple, and a soda. At the bottom of the box is a cherry Tootsie Pop and a note that says:

For your oral fixation.
Damon

"That's quite a friend you have there. Where can I sign up?" Trevor is like a bad rash, showing up when I least expect him, and impossible to get rid of.

"I'm not discussing my private life with you. Go read a book if you want dirt and smut. In fact, try *Bound*. You may enjoy it."

"I read it and loved it. I like the section on—"

I cover my ears. "Lalalalalala, I don't want to know." My brain can't fill with thoughts of Trevor and his lover when I want to imagine Damon.

"We need to get you hooked up with someone. You spend too much time trying to live vicariously through the fantasy life you've created for me."

"I know, girl. I've been high and dry for far too long. Maybe I'll hook up with someone on the opening night of Ahz. There will be a smorgasbord of eligible men, and I can't wait." He licks his lips provocatively.

I laugh at him because he's funny, but he's also smart and kind. Trevor has been a good mentor and friend, but he's lonely and looking for love like the rest of us. He has to work on his game.

"Trevor, how do other men know you're gay? I didn't pick up on it until you wanted to put the moves on Damon. Where do you meet men?"

"There are clubs and online dating sites, but they get old. I'm not looking for a one-night stand. I'm looking for the one."

"It's tough these days. So many people are happy with a casual hook-up. My mom used to say men wouldn't buy the cow if the milk was free. I get that, but don't you want to try the milk to make sure it's good? Anyway, I believe the perfect person will come along when the time is right. It seems to happen when you least expect it."

"Do you think Damon's the one?" He waggles his perfectly groomed brows.

"Argh, you're impossible. Always prying. Always probing. I'll say this: he's an amazing man, and for me, he's the one for right now. Now stop pestering me so I can call a man about a band."

The rest of the morning, I track down information about the likes and dislikes of Reluctant Capitalists. I reach their manager, who was helpful but brief. The only thing he said is the band likes single malt whiskey, preferably Redbreast 12 Year or Bushmills 16, and light beer on tap.

I talk to the event planner from their last concert who says the band prefers a private bartender and waitstaff on hand. They like cashmere blankets and down pillows for resting before and after the show. As for food, they were flexible, but she got the impression they like unique foods. The Kogi food truck comes to mind and would be the perfect catering option. And as long as we guarantee them more money than they'd make on a corner, I bet I could make that work. If not, we can get someone from Haywood's to bring food. The rest of the requests seem reasonable.

Trevor said they'd be difficult, but it's not like they are asking us for Skittles with the green ones removed.

I fill out the acquisition requests for the high-end whiskey, pillows, and blankets and make my way to Trevor's office to submit them. I'll run the food options by him, too.

I plop on the seat in front of his desk. "Here are the things I need for the band." I pass the acquisition forms across the neat-as-a-pin oak desk. "Can we talk about the food? Maybe go out for lunch?" I hate to leave my lunchbox, but wrapping up the menu is important, and if I can get it settled, then it's one more thing off my plate.

"Sure, what did you have in mind?"

"I thought about chasing down the Kogi truck. Have you ever had their stuff?"

"No, but I've heard it's good. How do we track it down?"

"I'll look at their Facebook page and see where they are today, or we can look at their tweets. I want you to try the food because it may be a good option for the band. If you like it, we can negotiate with Kogi to cater our event. What do you think?"

"Let me grab my keys. I'll drive while you navigate."

The truck sits on the corner of Sunset and Van Ness. The line winds down the street, but it only takes fifteen minutes for us to get to the front.

I order the short rib tacos, and Trevor gets spicy pork tacos and a kimchi quesadilla. There's no talking while we eat.

Trevor licks the last of the barbecue sauce from his fingers. "Holy shit, that was amazing. Who would have thought of mixing Korean barbecue and Mexican food? This is a great idea. There's no reason we can't offer both Kogi and Haywood's. Variety is the spice of life."

"Will you come meet the band to see how everything turns out?"

"Yes, but you're in charge of this part of the project and have to be there to make sure everything is running smoothly, so you'll meet the band too."

"You're kidding, right? Why me? Won't the team be jealous?"

"The team gets to go to the concert, but they didn't save the company nearly $100,000 in eight weeks. I borrow most of the team from marketing. So really, you're my team. You and me—we make the team."

"I like that." I raise my hand for a high five. "The dynamic duo."

"I'm Batman. You can be Robin," he says.

"I'm okay with that. I look amazing in red." I gather our garbage and throw it away.

Time to get back to work.

"Did you know we give a super saver award for cost cutting?" Trevor opens the car door while I get in. When he climbs behind the wheel, he turns and smiles. "I put you in for it. Most people would have taken that budget and had a field day shopping, but you spent your time getting donations. The stuff you finagled out of people astounds me. How did you do it?"

"I asked. It's as simple as that." I think about my talk with Em. Specifically, when she told me to ask Damon about his past. "I'm told, if you don't ask, you don't get." I'd do well to follow my advice.

"I don't know. There's something about you that people like. You make people feel at ease and comfortable. Hell, you have Damon wrapped around your little finger. I need some lessons, girl. You've got skills."

"I have no superpowers."

"Whatever." He turns onto the road back to the office. "Speaking of Damon, why didn't you have lunch with him today?"

I toss a dirty look at Trevor, but I know he'll never give up unless I let him into my inner circle.

With a huff, I turn to face him. "I'll cut you some slack because I like you, but I don't understand your obsession with Damon and me?"

"Inquiring minds want to know."

"Fine, I'll tell you what you want to know, but I never want to hear it come back to me."

Trevor grips the steering wheel in anticipation of a juicy story. Sadly, he's only getting the G-rated version.

"Damon and I met at a fundraiser. He asked me out, but I said no. We met for a book club and got to know each other better. We have lunch together, almost daily. We've been out to dinner several times, but haven't slept together, which is what you really want to know, and that's about it."

"Wow. My imagination is so much more interesting than your life. I hope he's into some kinky shit, like screwing on buses or something like that. He's the total Alpha male, and I don't want to hear he's the perfect gentleman."

"Sorry to disappoint you. He's a sexy, heterosexual, non-deviant man." I have a hard time keeping a straight face when I think about the steakhouse and the amazing office experience. I don't think I've begun to understand his deviant nature. I get lost in thoughts of the red scarf and what he might do with it.

"Earth to Kat." He uses my nickname, which pulls me from my daydream.

"Sorry." I got caught fantasizing about Damon—in front of Trevor. "What do you think about the band?"

"Good diversion, Ms. Cross. As far as the band is concerned, I love them. I think the drummer is hot. I could be happy feeling the beat of his stick against me. I'm sure he can pound out a good rhythm," he teases.

"Okay, here's the deal. You stop pestering me about Damon, and I'll do what I can to hook you up with the drummer. Since I have access to the band because of my generous boss, it's the least I can do."

"He's probably straight, but I appreciate the offer."

"He's not, and I'll make sure you're introduced properly. I'll serve you up like raw meat to a ravenous lion. Save your money because we're shopping before the grand opening."

"Look at you. Such a sleuth. How did you find out about the drummer?"

"I talked to the last event planner, and she told me the drummer, named Rylan, was not in his best form because of a recent breakup with his boyfriend, Tom. I then called the manager and asked him if we needed to make special arrangements for the band's significant others. He went through the list and confirmed Rylan was single."

"You're good. Okay, let's plan a shopping date, and you can choose my outfit, but I get to choose yours."

"Deal. Oh, and don't forget, I am graduating in ten days, so I won't be in that Monday. You're welcome to attend my ceremony."

"It's already on my calendar. I wouldn't miss it for the world."

The rest of the day ticks by slowly as time does when I want to be somewhere else. The weekend needs to start. I spend the last fifteen minutes organizing my desk. It's amazing how many ways I can accessorize with a phone, a notepad, and a vase of flowers. I look at my lunchbox and feel bad that I didn't eat what Damon gave me, but it's in the staff refrigerator for Monday.

Finally, the hour hand clicks into place, and I'm free.

The drive to Damon's takes me twenty minutes. I approach the gate and enter the code 0615 and wonder if there's any significance to the numbers. It hasn't escaped my attention that the grand opening of Ahz is on June fifteenth. Maybe that's the connection.

The farther up the driveway I go, the more nervous I feel.

Tonight is the night he and I will meet in the middle, so to speak. I've thought of nothing else all day except how his body will feel next to mine—inside of mine.

As I near the garage, I watch him approach wearing faded blue jeans and a white cotton button-down shirt with the sleeves rolled up. He's casual sexy, and I'm way overdressed in what Em picked out for me.

CHAPTER NINETEEN

I barely apply the emergency brake before he opens the door and practically pulls me from the car.

"It's been forever since I've seen you, and I've missed you. This feeling of longing is not a feeling I'm used to having." He hugs me, then steps back to stare. "I sat in my meeting all day today thinking of you. I couldn't stay in my desk chair because all I could imagine was your lips wrapped around me. I couldn't sit on the couch because it reminded me of my lips on you."

He reaches into the back seat and grabs my bag, then ushers me into the house. It smells delicious, like garlic and cheese, but the only thing I'm interested in is him.

"Damon, whatever plans you have need to wait. All I want to do is strip you naked and have my way with you."

He says nothing, but his eyes say everything. That dark, stormy look is back.

He drops my bag on the entryway floor and sweeps me from my feet to carry me upstairs. He sets me on my feet in the center of a massive room. I turn in circles, trying to take in what I see.

There's a massive king-sized bed with the duvet turned down, and a single rose lying across one pillow.

Flowers in vases sit everywhere, along with unlit candles placed beside the bed.

He thought of everything from the bottle of wine and glasses to the soft music playing in the background.

I hear something that sounds like, "Ahh," coming from him, and I stare in his direction.

"You look stunning. Unfortunately, you won't be needing these clothes tonight—except for those." He points to my black stilettos. "Later, I want you wearing those and nothing else, but right now, I'm going to make love to you until you scream my name."

Damon is so sure of himself, and it's such a turn-on. "I'm ready. Take me to bed."

It takes seconds for him to strip us both naked and press his body against mine. Guiding me backward, I retreat until I feel the bed against the back of my knees. With nowhere to go, I collapse, taking him with me.

We scoot up to the top, where the red rose lies across the pillow. He picks it up and trails it over my bare skin. The feel of the petals drifts across me, lighting up every nerve ending.

So many things go through my mind, but all I can focus on is how much I want him.

"Damon. Please!" I'm reduced to begging and pleading.

"I've thought about you begging, but I think you can be so much more convincing." He nips at my lips and licks a heated trail between my breast.

"Now, who's killing whom?"

"I'm bringing you to life."

I lie back and let whatever will happen, happen.

"AMAZING—ABSOLUTELY AMAZING," he declares as he caresses my body.

He pulls me to his side, so we face each other, and he looks at me with such tenderness.

I lay my head on the pillow and stare back. There isn't a male model who would look any better at this moment. Damon Noble is sex on fire.

"I agree. There's been so many firsts with you."

"Tell me about them."

I no longer feel embarrassed or shy with him. I share everything with him because he sees me like no one has.

"Well, first and foremost, you gave me my first orgasm during sex." If I had a blue ribbon, I would have stuck it to his chest. "Did you know orgasms feel different? Some are more intense than others. Don't get me wrong, they're all exceptional."

"Your first, huh?" He beams from ear to ear.

"I've given them to myself, but it's never happened with someone like this."

"I'm glad I could be of service. I'm more interested in knowing about how you pleasure yourself. I'd pay anything to watch that." He rises on his elbow and kisses me.

"No more discussions about self-gratification." My face heats at the thought of him watching.

"Why not? You talk about everything else so candidly. How did you ever grow up to be you? Most people would never talk so openly about the things you do."

"My parents were always upfront with me. If I was old enough to ask, I was old enough to know. No subject was ever taboo. I'm not embarrassed or ashamed to talk about most things because it seems normal. Honesty is important."

"I want to meet your parents. If they created you, they're amazing."

I can't tell if he's serious or teasing. "Do you seriously want to meet my parents?"

"Yes, I want to meet them." He rubs his hand from my ribs to my thigh, settling his palm on my hip.

"We can have lunch with them on Sunday. Or, you can wait and meet them at my graduation. You'll come, won't you?"

He nods. "I'll be there, and Sunday sounds great. Call them and make the arrangements. I'm happy to treat everyone to lunch."

"You don't have to take anyone to lunch. My mom will insist on fixing something. I can imagine what they'll say when I bring home a man."

"Haven't you brought a man to your parents' house before?"

"Yes, but it was over a year ago, and it was just a drive-by. I don't bring men home to meet my parents. It gives them the wrong impression. Warning, we'll have to set them straight as soon as we get there, or my mom will have me walking down the aisle."

His face goes from curious to concerned, then back to something resembling humor. He pulls me toward his chest, so my face presses against him. I inhale his scent; he's spicy, with undertones of lavender and cedar—intoxicating and sensual.

My hand covers his heart, and the pace speeds at my touch and taps out a steady cadence different from the one a few moments ago. I recognize it as his "I'm ready again" rhythm.

"Again? Already?"

"I told you we'd make love all night."

He rolls us both over and braces himself above me. The darn man delivers on his promise to make me scream his name.

I don't have a chance with him. I try my hardest to stay neutral and not fall in love, but it's impossible. I tumbled headfirst and failed to break my fall. Someday soon, I'll land, and it will hurt.

What Damon and I share is much more than sex. It feels like love, but that's impossible because Damon loves no one.

CHAPTER TWENTY

"Are you doing okay?" he asks

"Never felt better." My body aches, but my heart is full.

He rolls off the bed and strolls to a large walk-in closet, coming back with a long-sleeved dress shirt and a robe for me.

"Are you hungry?"

"Famished."

"Let's eat. Dinner is probably dry and awful, but it's sustenance, and you'll need it for tonight."

I take the shirt and put it on. It falls mid-thigh with the sleeves hanging past my hands by six inches.

He stands naked in front of me and buttons me up, leaving the top three undone. "I think this shirt will be my favorite from now on," he says. When he's done, he kisses me on the nose.

At his chest of drawers, he pulls out a pair of sweatpants. As he steps into them, every muscle in his torso flexes when he lifts his legs into the body-hugging fabric. The soft cotton clings to him, like a jealous lover, making me envious of those sweatpants.

"What are you thinking about?"

"How nice it would be to be your sweatpants."

He laughs and takes a last lingering look at the bed before leading me out of his room.

"We need to get out of here immediately, or we may never leave," he says.

I follow him downstairs and into the enormous kitchen.

He opens the oven and pulls out what appears to be chicken Kiev. It's dry but still edible.

"Where are the dishes? I'll set the table." Looking around, I ask, "Do you want to eat at the island or the table?"

He directs me to the dishes and silverware, and we sit at the island.

I serve up the chicken while he pulls a pre-made salad from the refrigerator. We each take a seat and eat in silence. I'd give him all my pennies for his thoughts.

"We were talking about firsts earlier, but we got distracted. What are your other firsts with me?" he asks.

"I already said the orgasms, so that one's covered. I've never given or received oral pleasure, so that's another. I've never fooled around in unconventional places like a restaurant booth or an executive office. You're a bad influence. You've ruined me, and I'll never be good for anyone else now that I've had you."

His expression turns from happy-go-lucky to serious. Tension sits in the air like thick fog.

"What's wrong?"

He stares at me—almost through me. There's something brewing inside him. He pours two glasses of wine and drains his in one gulp.

I reach over to hold his hand, but he avoids my touch and instead grasps the bottle and fills his glass again. I have no idea what changed his mood, but he's brooding over something. His eyes are no longer alight with passion but clouded with pain.

"Would you like more wine?" he asks.

His question is an attempt to avoid dealing with the issue at hand, whatever that may be.

"No," I respond. No longer feeling blissful but soiled by his sour mood, I say, "I'd love answers, and if I can't have those, I'll take a shower."

He turns the wineglass in circles and watches the liquid move. "You can use my bathroom. Do you remember how to find it, or do you need me to show you?"

"I can find it." I jump off the stool and turn to leave but stop. "Whatever just happened here wasn't warranted. Whoever you're thinking about. Whoever you're mad at, I'm not her."

My statement catches him off guard, but I don't wait for him to reply. I walk to the hallway, grab my bag, and stomp up the stairs. I can be mad too.

Now that I'm alone in his bedroom, I take a few minutes to look around. I didn't get to truly see anything earlier because he distracted me. For the first time, I see the dark furniture and luxurious bedding that is posh but masculine with its brown and gold palette. I didn't notice the wall of glass. His house sits so far up in the canyon, it's like sitting in a tree house. Maybe it reminds him of his father and brother and the beloved tree house they built and shared.

The bathroom is unbelievable, with a shower made to hold no less than ten people. Heads and jets spray from every wall. There's even a button for steam. It takes a few minutes to figure out how to turn everything on, but I finally get the water adjusted and climb into a new experience.

The jets are set for Damon's height, so a lot of the water shoots over my head, but the heat and steam relax my muscles as I sink against the far wall. One side of the shower contains a bench, and on it is a wide selection of body washes and shampoos. Looking through them, I find the least manly of the bunch and lather up.

"Can I wash your back?"

His voice startles me, and I spin around to see him.

"I'm sorry." The whispered apology drips with sincerity. He wraps his arms around me, and he tugs me close.

"You don't have to be sorry, but we need to talk about whatever takes you to that place. This isn't the first time you've gone there."

He sits on the bench and pulls me to his lap. We sit together as the water pours over us and prunes our skin. My head leans lazily against his shoulder as he cradles me in his arms. When the water runs cold and I shiver, he rises with me in his arms, turns off the water, and carries me out of the shower.

Setting me down on the soft rug, he rushes to the linen cabinet, pulls out a large bath towel, and drapes me in it. He has a second one he wraps around his waist.

I have a hard time separating this man from the angry one in the kitchen. If I'm honest, that man rarely shows up, but when he does, it is an unsettling experience.

We move to the glass wall in the bedroom and take a seat on the overstuffed chairs. The stars light up the night sky.

"I can't imagine you with another man," he says.

I'm jolted from my peaceful moment and catapulted back to the here and now.

"You don't have to picture me with another man. I'm here with you." I reach for his hand.

"You are now, but what about tomorrow or next week or next month?"

"Damon, you made it clear you were not ready for a relationship. You wanted to start slow. We agreed to take it one kiss at a time."

"We are way beyond kisses, Katarina. The minute I sank myself into you, everything changed. I don't know why, but it did, and I need to know you're mine."

I leave my chair and climb onto his lap. "I'm yours if that's what you want. Is that what you really want?"

"I want you, and I'm ready to move forward. You brand me with your kisses. You mesmerize me with your laughter. You astonish me with your candor. And you completely paralyze my heart with your ability to love." He plays with a strand of my wet hair. "A while back, you told me I was lovable and worthy, and I didn't agree. I still don't think I deserve your love, but I want it. I need it."

Tears pool in my eyes. His words are heartfelt and earnest, and my heart somersaults in my chest.

"Don't cry." He wipes my tears and muffles my sobs with a kiss. "I never want to make you cry."

"They're good tears. I never expected those words to come out of your mouth."

"I guess there's hope for me yet," he says with a small smile. "It's getting late. Are you ready to go to bed?"

His strong arms carry me to the massive bed, where he lays me on the soft sheets and slides next to me. His chin sits comfortably above my shoulder with his breath tickling my neck, sending small shivers down my spine. I know his intent is to climb into bed and sleep, but having him next to me makes that damn near impossible.

We make love once more before sleep pulls us under.

CHAPTER TWENTY-ONE

Light pours through the windows, and like a cat, I stretch, causing every muscle to cry out in rebellion. Damon lies next to me, head propped on his elbow, hair mussed up, and ready for more.

"Good morning. How did you sleep?"

"Like the dead. How long have you been up?"

"Less than an hour." He brushes his thumb across my lips. "Watching you sleep is my new favorite pastime." He kisses my forehead, then nose, and finally my lips. "I made coffee. Do you want some?"

"Sure. I can get it."

He rolls over and picks up a white carafe from the nightstand.

"I've got it. Black with a dash of cream, right?"

"How do you remember? We only had coffee together a few times."

"It's all in the details." He pours and doctors a cup. "Once you have coffee, I'll fix you breakfast. I make a mean omelet."

He hands me the cup and slides back into bed next to me.

"Are you worn out?" His eyes are alight with a fiery passion.

"Not enough to stop."

"Oh, my girl is insatiable."

"Your girl is hungry."

"Come on." He climbs out of bed and starts for the door. "You can't live off sex alone."

No, but I'm willing to try.

DAMON MAKES an excellent omelet that we enjoy on the deck out back. The view of the canyon is breathtaking. It's hard to believe we're only twenty minutes outside the city.

After cleaning up our dishes, I get a tour of the house. It spans three floors, each containing a large deck. As we enter the theater, I'm amazed at how much it looks like an actual cinema. There's a concession stand with a popcorn machine and a glass case that contains everything from Whoppers to Sour Patch Kids.

"The movie came yesterday."

"How did you do that? You must have some incredible connections."

"It's true what they say, that it's not always what you know, but often who you know that's more important. I was thinking we could invite Anthony and Emma if you want."

"Is it okay if we don't this time? This is our first weekend together, and I don't want to share you with anyone."

"It's a deal, but don't forget to call your parents about tomorrow. Sadly, I already told my mother we'd stop by after lunch for a quick visit today. I hope that's okay."

"Of course, it's okay. What time are we going there?"

"Not for a few hours. We have time for *other things* if you're interested."

"You can persuade me to do *other things.*"

Damon and I spend the next two hours making love on every surface we could lie on, kneel on, or stand on. Nothing was exempt.

We started downstairs on the pool table and ended upstairs on the kitchen counter, with lawn chairs, desks, and benches in-between. When we couldn't take any more, we dragged our sore bodies up the stairs and got ready for the visit with his mother.

Unpacking my bag, I pull out the red scarf and set it on the bed. Damon looks at the scarf. "We'll need that later." The way he says it makes me warm all over. He walks to the corner and picks up my black stilettos. "We'll need these, too."

Heat rushes from my chest to my face.

"Don't worry, I know your boss, and I can get him to cut you some slack if you need a day to recover." He winks, then goes to the bathroom to prepare our shower.

We take a long, leisurely shower, enjoying the simple pleasure of lathering and rinsing each other. He washes my hair and detangles it with his conditioner.

Stepping out, we dry one another before he reaches for my brush and pulls it from my crown to the ends. I've never had a man brush my hair—it is another first and feels so much better when someone else does it. The bristles of my brush massage my scalp as he gently strokes the tangles free.

"Your hair is soft and silky and always smells good." He lifts my wet hair and brings it to his nose. "Now you smell like me."

"Which is good because you smell amazing too. What cologne do you wear?"

"Something from D & G that my mom gives me every Christmas."

"I like it."

He dresses and excuses himself to take care of emails and phone calls while I spend the next thirty minutes getting ready to visit his mom.

We arrive around one o'clock, and Rose has hugs for both of us and a kiss for Damon.

"It's so good to see you two together again."

"It's good to see you, too." What I want to say but can't is we've been inseparable since yesterday.

Keeping my thoughts in my head and away from my mouth, I follow Damon to the courtyard, where Rose set out iced tea and snacks.

Damon guides me to the settee and grins when he sees how slow I sit. Next to me, he lifts my hand and places it in his lap.

His mother misses nothing and smiles warmly at the show of affection.

"Damon, be a good son and go to the cellar to grab a bottle of the Italian wine you like so much. I want to send it home with Katarina."

He eyes his mom but does her bidding. Before he turns the corner, he says, "Behave yourself."

Rose laughs at his attempt to censure her.

"I knew the day I met you, you'd be good for him. He's being a gentleman, right? I ask because he can be pushy and demanding."

"He's always a gentleman, patient, and accommodating."

"Really? You must make him happy. It's been entirely too long since I've seen him carefree and content. Those other girls drove me nuts. I know one of them is your roommate, and she's pleasant enough, but all the other girls were mere distractions." She looks over her shoulder in the direction Damon disappeared. "He'll be back soon, but I wanted to let you know how happy I am you two are seeing one another. Don't let him bully you. He'll try but push back. The Noble men are strong and stubborn, which means you need to be stronger."

"What's this about stubborn, Mother?" Damon arrives carrying a bottle of merlot.

"Your mother said that stubbornness runs in your family, and I told her I hadn't seen that trait yet, but I'll be on the lookout for it."

"In my twenty-nine years, I've learned one thing, and that's you don't argue with a group of women. It never goes well."

"Smart man," I reply.

"Tell me how things are going with the new club?" Rose asks.

He gives his mom the details about the last-minute fixes and extravagant opening night festivities. He proudly tells her what a great job I've done with the gift bags, making me feel good about my accomplishment.

"Do you like working at Noble, Katarina? Is it everything you thought it would be?"

I look at him, then back at Rose before I answer.

"It's turned out to be more than I could have hoped for. I finish my internship there the week of the opening. It's been a great experience, and I've learned so much from Trevor. I'm sure everything I've worked on will help me find a permanent job."

"I'm confident you'll do well in the job market," she says. "What else do you have planned for the weekend?"

I look at Damon because I don't know what we have planned.

"Katarina and I are doing a little shopping, then dinner, and a movie. Tomorrow, we're having supper with her parents."

Rose's eyes grow in surprise, then a smile spreads across her face.

"That sounds wonderful." She points to my bag. "Put my number in your phone, so you can call me next week, and we can meet for lunch."

"Katarina has lunch with me," Damon says in a purely possessive manner.

"Nonsense, you can live without her for a day." Rose recites her number, and I plug it into my phone before we're off.

He drives a few blocks down the street, then turns left. Halfway down the block, he pulls into a driveway where a large white colonial house sits in the center of an enormous lot. It's hard to believe anyone still owns space like this in Los Angeles.

"Where are we?"

"We're at my childhood home. Follow me. I want to show you something."

He takes my hand and leads me around the side of the house to the backyard.

In the center is a massive oak tree with the coolest tree house I've ever seen. There are several levels, each attached with ladders and ropes. Tattered blue curtains blow in the breeze.

"Come and look. This is where I spent nearly all my childhood."

I can't believe we're sneaking into someone else's tree house. "If we get caught, I'm placing all the blame on you."

"Fine." He takes my hand and, like an excited kid, tugs me toward the tree house.

I want to say no, but I feel his excitement, and he's sharing an intimate part of his life with me, so I forge on.

He reaches down and removes my heels before he places my hands on the ladder and climbs up behind me. We take one rung at a time, with him nipping at my behind. Once at the top, I'm in awe of the place. A kid could get lost up here.

It's a fantasy come true. There are spyglasses and a telescope. In the corner is a treasure chest full of who knows what.

Wooden benches line one side. He guides me to it and forces me to sit. He kneels in front of me and glides his hands up my thighs. The action lifts my dress high on my legs.

"Damon, stop. This house belongs to some kid. As enticing as it sounds, I don't want to get caught with my pants down up here."

"Relax, Angel, this house belongs to me, and it's on my list of places to take you. I want you, and I want you here."

How can I say no to that? The man has a fantasy of making love to me in a tree house. Who am I to crush his dreams?

It doesn't take long for both of us to find our pleasure.

I lean back and look at the ceiling. Carved into the plywood above my head are three sets of initials: SN, RN, and DN.

He follows my line of sight. "Lots of childhood memories."

AS WE PULL out of the driveway, I reach over to take his hand.

"How many girls did you bring up to that tree house when you were a boy?" I ask teasingly.

"None. Girls weren't allowed Not even my mom has been in it. There are three sets of initials on the ceiling. They're the only people who've been there: my dad, my brother, and me. You're the first girl up there as long as you don't count the scores of Penthouse magazines stashed in the treasure chest." He squeezes my hand. "When we have more time, I'll take you on a tour of the main house."

"Why do you keep the house if you won't live in it?"

"It's a house built for a family, not for a bachelor. I keep it because I can't let go. I'm not ready yet."

I don't pry. We all have things we're not ready to let go of. I still have a collection of Barbies and also kept the collar to the first dog we ever had. Bubbles passed away when I was fifteen, but I could never part with that collar.

"Where are we going?"

"Shopping for underwear."

"What do you have against mine? If you take them, someone will see my goodies."

"No one is allowed to see your goodies but me, which is why we're buying an obscene amount of underwear. That way, I won't feel bad when I'm compelled to keep a pair or two or three."

The thought makes me wiggle in my seat.

"Stop squirming, or I might take a detour."

"Aren't you tired of me yet?"

"Never. Are you tired of me?"

"Nope. I'm just getting started with you, Mr. Noble."

Damon takes me to an exclusive lingerie shop on Rodeo Drive. He insists on watching me while I try everything on. I walk out of the store with two bags of tiny strips of fabric. They cover very little, but it doesn't matter because they won't last a second with him around.

"Now where?"

"You gave me an idea. I want to try something out."

"Shall I say goodbye to the underwear I have on?"

"Most definitely." He speeds toward our destination. As we pull into the garage at Ahz, I can only imagine what he has planned.

We enter, and Damon has a discussion with security. His smile is so big. I can't imagine what he has envisioned, but whatever it is, it makes him happy.

Eventually, I find myself on the sixth floor with the music playing and the lights flashing. We hold each other and dance to the sounds of K-Ci and JoJo as the song *All My Life* plays through the sound system.

I stare at the floor below us. "Damon, people can see me."

"Shh. No one can see you. Security has cleared the building, and they shut off the security feed. It's private. Come here. I want to dance with my girlfriend on the glass floor of my club."

"You just called me your girlfriend. You know what I said about flattery?"

"No, tell me again," he says.

"Flattery will get you nowhere, but sweet words will get you whatever you want on the glass floor in your club."

He jumps up and throws his fist in the air. "Yes!"

He reaches below my dress and with a single tug, my underwear fall from my body.

"Damon."

"You said whatever I want." He drops to his knees and pleasures me to the beat of the music. Damon is a man of many skills—oral being near the top. Once the last quiver leaves my body, Damon stands and holds me while we sway to several more songs.

He kisses me and tells me he'll be right back. A minute later, I look through the glass into the VIP lounge, where Damon smiles from below.

I laugh, lift my dress, and dance for him.

When he returns, he confesses, "That was awesome. I'll never be able to be in the VIP lounge and not think of you on the floor above me. If I died today, I'd die a happy man."

"I might die if you don't feed me soon. I get grumpy if I don't eat." I look at him and push my lips out into a pout.

"How about In-N-Out? We can take it home and watch the movie."

"Perfect. I want a double-double with fries and a chocolate shake."

He gives a look of surprise.

"Don't look at me like that. I've been exercising from morning to nightfall for two days now, and I'm famished."

"You have to be hungry. I exercise all the time, and you've worn me out. I think the scarf and heels will have to wait for another day." We take the elevator to the first floor. "I think you're trying to kill me."

"Who wanted to make love in a tree house and dance on a glass floor?"

He raises his hand, "Guilty. I can't get enough of you. The glass floor was a sight to behold. Next time I want you naked."

"Fat chance of that."

"Is that a challenge?"

The one thing I know is Damon always rises to a challenge.

WE TAKE our dinner to the theater and watch the new release he scored, then snuggle on the couch and enjoy a peaceful night together.

Exhausted from the physical demands of pleasing each other, we trudge to his bed and collapse. Lying next to Damon feels so natural. He's my person.

"I'm falling in love with you," I admit cautiously. I don't know how he'll respond, but I know it's something that needs saying. I can't fall further and expect to survive.

Pulling me as close as possible, he tells me, "I love your love, and I'll do my best to be worthy. My life is better because you're in it."

It's not an affirmation of love, but it may be as close as I'll get from him. Actions speak louder than words, and Damon's actions say he cares. I fall asleep with his breath on my neck and my heart in his hands.

CHAPTER TWENTY-TWO

"Should I fear meeting your parents?" Damon asks.

Stuck in traffic on Interstate 210, we have plenty of time to talk. Normally it's the 405 that's bottlenecked, so it's odd we're at a complete stop.

"You should be terrified. I don't come from the average American family. My parents are way ahead of their time, but they're traditional and old-fashioned in many ways. I couldn't date until I was sixteen, and everyone had to meet my dad before I went anywhere with them. He made copies of their identification cards so he could track them down if I disappeared."

"Thank goodness I brought my ID. They may even let me leave the house with you," he teases.

"These days, I'm on my own. Once I went off to college, they figured they'd done their job. If I didn't know how to care for myself by then, then I'd succumb to natural selection."

"You're joking, right? I've never met a daddy that didn't obsess over his little girl's safety."

"Dad worries about my safety, but he trusts me to make good decisions."

We inch along on the freeway until we come across an awful car accident. With the amount of mangled metal on the side of the road, no one survived.

"That's a bad one," Damon says.

"I hate the traffic in Los Angeles. People get distracted so easily with cell phones and other stuff. Accidents happen when people don't pay attention."

We sit in silence for a few minutes. Once we clear the accident, the freeway opens up, and it's smooth sailing.

"Tell me, have you met a lot of fathers?"

Has he always been cool and confident, or does he ever waver under pressure?

"I've only met one girl's father. He was okay. Since then, I wouldn't call what I do dating. You're my first date in ten years."

"You can choose not to answer, but who's this girl who broke your heart?"

He stares ahead and bites the inside of his cheek, causing it to hollow. I wish he'd open up. It would be so much easier to have a battle against a known enemy.

"Mara was my first and only girlfriend before you. All I'll say is, she was unfaithful, and it destroyed me."

I take his hand and squeeze. I can't imagine what it would feel like to give your love and trust to someone, only to have them betray you. Infidelity would ruin me.

"I'm sorry. I promise to never invalidate our relationship by being unfaithful. I'm yours, and only yours."

His large hand wraps around mine to bring it to his lips for a kiss.

"What else do I need to know about your family?"

It is sweet that he wants to make a good impression.

"The best way to earn my family's respect is to be honest. Engage in conversation and enjoy yourself. They have no filters, so don't be surprised at how inappropriate they can be. Everyone says exactly what they're thinking or feeling. Out of the bunch, I'm the most reserved, and that's not saying much. For example, penises were the topic at dinner for Thanksgiving last year. How you end up talking about man sausage during turkey dinner is beyond me, but it happened. We ended the conversation when my brother thought vaginas should get equal billing."

"I agree with your brother. Only I'd push for top billing."

Damon doesn't know what he's in for. Going to my home is like entering a clown car. You'll make it alive, but it will be an experience.

"If they're like you, I'll like them just fine."

"They're like me, but on steroids. Pay close attention, or they'll bulldoze you."

"Okay. I'll try to keep up."

Mom must have heard the roar of Damon's tricked-out Mustang pull into the driveway.

She walks toward us, drying her hands on the kitchen towel tucked into the waist of her jeans. Once we exit, she gives me a bear hug, then walks straight to Damon to say hello.

"This is the Viking god you were telling me about? Katarina, you were right. He is every inch as beautiful as you described. Turn around, Damon, and let me see the whole package."

He looks at me incredulously as his forehead creases, and one of his brows raises to his hairline

I bite the insides of my cheeks to hold back a smirk and give him an I-told-you-so look.

He nonchalantly turns as told. His blue jeans hug his body, showing what he's working with while his yellow shirt squeezes his chest, displaying finely tuned muscles. The sleeves stretch over his beautiful biceps—the same biceps that flexed above me this morning.

"Do I pass inspection, Mrs. Cross?"

"Oh, yes, you'll do. I love a little eye candy at the table. It makes the meal sweeter."

"Leave him be, Mom. He's been here for less than five minutes, and you've made him an ornament at the table. Come on, Damon. Time to meet the other comedian who raised me."

My father and brother are in the living room.

"When did you decide to come to dinner?" I ask Chris.

"When I found out you were bringing a boy home, little sister."

"Damon is hardly a boy. What about you? When are you going to bring a boy home for dinner?"

"I'll bring one home when I find one worthy of me. I'm not easy, and I'm not cheap."

"Good for you. Set your standards high," I tell him.

The rest of the afternoon goes much like the beginning. Everyone sizes up Damon and asks him inappropriate questions.

My dad and brother take turns grilling him about his intentions, and to Damon's credit, he stands on his own two feet, dishing it back as fast as my family can serve it up.

"Does anyone want more? Maybe something sinful?" Mom asks.

Looking into Damon's eyes, I see he's struggling to contain his laughter.

This has piqued my mom's curiosity. "Is there something I should know?"

"You know your daughter. Sometimes her appetite can't be sated."

"Really? I've never known her to be a glutton." She stands. "Is that a yes or no on dessert?"

We opt for a tour of the house instead. It isn't that big and doesn't take long to make the rounds. We finish the excursion in my bedroom, where I close the door and grab him by his shirt. Fisting handfuls of cotton, I drag him toward me and pull him to my twin bed.

"Should we be on your bed like this in your parents' house?" His uneasiness makes me giggle.

"If my dad finds you in my bed, he'll kill you, but isn't that what you like? The thrill of the unknown?"

"I'd like to live a little longer."

"No worries. I'm nearly twenty-four, and my parents aren't coming in to check on us. Let's make out on my bed, and then on Emma's."

"Emma's bed? The other twin is hers?"

We lie on my bed, and I try to explain why Emma has a bed in my room.

"Once her mom died, she only had her dad. He was a truck driver and gone a lot. Emma lived with us throughout her middle school and high school years. My mom eventually bought her a bed so we could share a room like sisters."

I rolled over and kissed him until he moaned.

"The louder you are, the more likely my dad will come to investigate."

"I'd take one for the team."

"I totally love you." Holy shit, I loved him—everything about him, from the scent of his body to the taste of his skin to the feel of his hands on my body. I love the way confidence oozes from every pore and the fact that he's dependable yet unpredictable. I love Damon Noble.

"You're crazy." He kisses me again. Only this time, he makes a lot of noise; none of it authentic. "I'd take any beating your dad would give me just to be with you."

"I appreciate that you'd take a beating for me, but there's no risk of getting caught. My parents take a walk after dinner every night. They take forty-three minutes from start to finish."

"What about your brother?"

He tickles me until I nearly bust a gut.

"My brother is oblivious. Besides, he's tuned into 60 *Minutes*."

"I'm not good with this subject, but your brother bats for my team, right?"

"You are astute. Was it the talk of bringing boys home or his feminine swagger?" I settle next to him with my head on his chest. "He came out several years ago. It wasn't a big deal with my family. We all knew and gave him time to figure it out himself. That's the one thing I love about my family. There's never been any pressure to be anything other than what we already were."

"You're very lucky."

"I am. My parents challenge us to be better and do better. They demand nothing from us, except that we live our lives with honesty and integrity. Growing up with these values allows my brother to live his life being true to himself. It is powerful having that unconditional love, as you know, because your mother loves you the same."

"My mother loves me, but she has no choice. I'm the only one left."

"Oh, Damon. Someday you'll tell me why you think you're so unlovable, and I'll tell you why you're wrong."

We straighten ourselves and find Chris exactly where I thought he'd be —sitting in front of the massive flat-screen TV watching the news.

"You two came up for air. That was quick." Chris eyes Damon as if to say, *Sorry, man.*

Damon has no idea what to say. If he defends himself, he all but admits we were up to no good. If he doesn't defend himself, he owns the put-down.

I ride in on my white steed and save my man.

"Sometimes quality is so much better than quantity. It turns me on knowing I can get my man to the point of no return lickety-split." I take my tongue and let it linger slowly as I circle my lips.

"Touché, sis. So, Damon, what do I have to do to get an invitation to Ahz? Does you sleeping with my sis get me benefits?"

"I'll send you an invitation, but not because you're trying to pimp your sister out, but because you'll fit right in with my target audience."

"Wow, someone is finally catering to the strapping young gay population of the world? Normally, we're in the basement or back-alley clubs."

"I'm not opening a gay club. I'm opening a club that, no matter what your gender preference is, you are encouraged to attend and enjoy yourself."

"I thought you'd tell me I was encouraged to come. I was getting excited about that."

"Stop flirting with my boyfriend. Go find your own," I say.

"No worries. I have the lickety down, but I'm not a fan of the split."

Damon looks back and forth between us. I warned him, but I don't think he believed me. Minutes later, my parents return, which saves Damon from the inevitable ribbing he'd get from my brother.

"What's on your agenda for the rest of the afternoon?" Mom asks.

"Not much. I have laundry to do, a paper to edit, and I need to iron my gown for graduation. I need things I left at Damon's house, and I want to read the next few chapters of *Bound*."

"Oh, I love that book," Mom says. "I tried to get your dad to read it, but he wasn't interested. What about you, Damon? Are you interested?"

"Katarina and I are reading it together. We have our own private book club. We meet on Wednesdays to discuss the week's chapters, and I find the story interesting and the characters familiar," he says to my mother as he looks at me.

"I bet you two have some interesting conversations. How is Emma? I haven't heard from her in a few weeks. I hope she's okay?"

"She's seeing a man named Anthony. You'll meet him at our graduation."

"Is she still selling her time, or has she given that up now that she's graduating? How does one put 'professional escort' on a résumé?"

"I don't know. Maybe 'excellent interpersonal skills' or 'flexible scheduling'?" I could sell anything. "She closed up shop as soon as she and Anthony became an item. Damon has been friends with him for a while, and says he's a good guy, so I trust that he is."

"That's good to know. She's like a daughter to me," Mom says.

I hate to leave, but there's so much to do.

"We have to head out, Mom, but I'll see you next Monday."

We say our goodbyes and head home. Damon looks relaxed and carefree.

"What did you think of my family?"

"I love your family. I can see why you are you. They lay it out there. Your brother is funny, and I'm happy to invite him to the grand opening. Is he dating anyone? I only ask for invitation purposes."

"Thanks for clarifying. I'd hate to be tossed aside for my brother," I tease. "He's not a dating kind of guy. He's still in his trying-everyone-out phase. One day he'll find the right guy and settle down, but until then, I think we can all agree he's a man-whore."

"How did you get to twenty-three unscathed?"

"My mom said to take care of myself, and if I give myself to a man, I should make sure he's worthy of me. I wish I could say the first two were, but I don't lie. I had nothing to compare their worth to until I met you."

"Let's go by your place and get some of your things so you can stay with me. The last two nights have been amazing, and I don't want to be without you. What do you say? Bring your laundry and your gown. My housekeeper can take care of all that for you."

"You have a housekeeper?"

"Yes, she comes in Monday through Friday. If you stay tonight, you can meet her in the morning. She'll be thrilled to have something else to do."

"How many of your sleepovers has she met?"

"I don't have sleepovers. You're the first and only woman who's been in my house besides my mom and Claire, the housekeeper. It's like my tree house. Entrance is by personal invite only."

That comes as quite a surprise. I'm the only woman who's slept in his bed, showered in his shower, and sat at his breakfast bar. I smile, knowing that for whatever reason, I made it on Damon's VIP list.

"Where did you have sex before me?" I hope he doesn't say in the booth at a restaurant. I want those moments we shared to be something special, not something he does with all the girls.

"Mostly hotels, sometimes their places. Back then, it was purely physical. Now it's for survival. What do you say? Will you stay?"

"I'll stay if we can revisit the scarf and heels?"

"Deal. I have a few ideas for those." He waggles his brows in a comedic gesture.

"I was thinking about the book. What would you say if I wanted to try some things from it?" Experimenting with Damon doesn't scare me.

"I told you earlier I'm always open to experimentation. Just don't ask me to abuse you."

"There's no risk of that, but I thought we could write the things interesting to us down on a piece of paper and put them in a bag. Each time we meet, we pick one and try it. What do you think?"

"I'm in. We have about one hundred and fifty pages left in the book, so let's agree to do fifty pages a week so we can finish in three weeks."

"Are you in a hurry?" I ask.

"Yes, I want to get to the little pieces of paper."

I shake my head. "I don't know how I ended up at this place with you, but I'm glad I'm here. The day you picked me up for the hospital benefit, you looked right through me. I didn't think you found me attractive at all. What changed your mind?"

"I looked over and saw the most beautiful woman dressed in red, and you took my breath away. When we entered the car and your dress rode up your leg, I was speechless. You have incredible legs. I stared at you all night, wondering what it was about you that was different."

"Did you ever figure it out?"

"I have a theory. I think the universe brought you to me. All sorts of things happened to put you in my path, and I can't ignore that. Have you wondered why you haven't met the right person yet?"

"Because I was waiting for you?" My answer sounds more like a question than a statement. "I think we're meant for each other." We sit in contemplative silence for the duration of the trip.

At my house, I pack a few things and leave a note on the table for Em. I tuck *Bound* into my bag before we go.

Snuggled on his tan leather couch, he reads *Bound* while I put the finishing touches on my term paper.

He startles me when he jumps up and races to the kitchen, only to return with two pens and two notepads. He slides next to me, and I watch him write note after note, folding each in half when he finishes.

"Are you having fun yet, Mr. Noble?"

"Not yet, but I plan to once we start our book review. I'm warming up to your idea of doing things by the book."

"Should I be scared?"

"You should be terrified," he says, repeating the words I told him earlier. The corners of his mouth tip into a smile.

He closes his book and leaves me to read on my own while he checks email and makes a few phone calls from his office. Forty minutes later, he's back with two glasses of wine and a sexy smirk.

"How's the book coming?" he asks. "Did you read anything interesting?"

I pick up a handful of notes to show him how busy I've been. He disappears and returns with a Ziploc storage bag. Placed in the bag, our sexual fantasies are zipped tight for future use.

"Let's go upstairs. I ran a bath and thought we can enjoy it together before we go to bed."

Bubbles pop and candles flicker while I sip my wine and relax against Damon.

"I want to do this every night with you." He cups a handful of water and drizzles it over my breasts. "Move your things in and share my world."

Who is this man behind me? Two months ago, he didn't date. He didn't have relationships, and he wasn't looking to have someone share his world.

"I don't know what to say."

"Say, yes. We're good together."

"I'd love to say yes, but I can't. Not right now. I need to give Emma time to find a new roommate and figure out what I'll do to support myself. I've barely gotten used to the idea of being your girlfriend." I turn to face him, but water sloshes out of the tub, and I stay put. "There's nothing I want more than to be with you every minute of every day, but I'm not willing to give up my space yet. Let's compromise. We can stay here several days a week and stay at my place several days a week. We'll take one day each week to be on our own. I don't want you tiring of me."

"I'd rather have you here with me every day, but I'll take you any way I can get you. Is there room in your closet for a few of my suits?"

"I'll make room." What will it feel like to have his suits next to my dresses? Sharing closet space is a huge step.

We dry off and enter the bedroom. On the bed is my red scarf. My head swings to where he stands, and I realize 'go to bed' didn't mean 'go to sleep.' He tugs at the towel, and it drops to the floor, pooling around my feet. Naked except for a smile, he takes me to the plate-glass window and stands me in front of it. On the floor next to my feet are my black heels. I step into both and take my place in front of the window with the trees and starry night as my backdrop.

"Do you remember the day at the Mongolian barbecue place

when you trussed yourself up to tease me? Let's see how strong this scarf is."

I follow his directions and raise my hands while he creates a knot only a Boy Scout would know.

His torment begins at my shoes and ends at my mouth. God bless the book club.

CHAPTER TWENTY-THREE

"Good afternoon, Ms. Cross. Head on in, he's on the phone, but I'm sure he'll be off in a minute. I ordered you both Asian chicken salads. I hope that sounds okay."

"It's perfect, Greta. You're the best."

Inside Damon's office, I walk to the table where lunch sits and take a seat. He continues with a contentious call. His brows furrow while his lips stretch into a grim line. His face is red, starting as a shade of pink at his chin and ending blood-red near his hairline.

The vein that runs down the center of his forehead pulses, which means he's furious. When he sees me focusing on him, he swings his chair and gives me his back, but I can still hear him yelling under his breath.

"I told you to stop calling me. I'm not interested. Go to hell, Mara." He hangs up and growls.

Mara ... shit. I didn't expect that, and by Damon's expression, he didn't either.

"Should I leave? Do you need time alone to calm down and think?"

"No. If you left, I'd be more stressed. Let me kiss you, and I'll be fine."

The minute our tongues meet, I know staying was the right decision. My hands stroke his shoulders until he relaxes beneath my fingertips.

"I don't know what I'd do if I couldn't see you every day. I want you every minute. When we're together, I think about you. When we're apart, I'm obsessed with you. Tonight will be a living hell not being able to spend the night wrapped around you."

Tonight is Chinese food with Em. "It's good to spend time with our friends. Why don't you call Anthony and hang out? If Em is with me, that means Anthony is by himself."

"You're right. I know you need your space."

"I don't need space from you, but I need to see my friends. Why don't we plan on having dinner with Emma and Anthony soon? That way, we won't have to live without each other at all."

He hangs his head. "I'll call him after our lunch and make plans."

After lunch, I finish my day with Trevor and head home for girly time with Em.

"IS HE A SHOW-ER OR A GROWER?" she asks as she serves up the Chinese food.

We haven't seen each other in what seems like weeks, although it's only been days.

"Definitely a grower."

She shoves a piece of orange chicken in her mouth and talks around it. "I love a grower. You never know what you'll end up with." She swallows and continues. "It's like those little sponge animals that become massive once you add water. With a show-er, it's all out there, and often it's never as good as it looks. Has it been good?"

"We're basically living together because we can't get enough of each other."

"I got you, girl. It's the same with Anthony and me. Let's gorge on Chinese food and compare notes."

The situation with Damon and the call I walked in on has been bothering me all day. I called Em as soon as I got to my desk. Who better to ask than my bestie? When she answered, I gave her the details and asked, "Do you think I should worry about this girl named Mara?"

"You said he yelled at her and told her he wasn't interested, so I wouldn't worry. Besides, he's with you, not with her. You should ask him about her. You have a right to know."

"Do I? I'm not sure I have a right to his past when all I'm interested in is his future. What's that saying about opening a can of worms? I don't want to unleash something I'm not prepared to handle, or he's not ready to deal with."

"Don't be a coward. She's the can of worms that placed herself and the can opener on his table. She has no place at your table."

Em has a way with words that confuses me and inspires me, but she's right. There is no room for Mara in our life.

We snuggle on the couch like we did as kids. She hogs the blanket, and I lean on her shoulder.

She picked the movie *Dirty Dancing* because it's one of our all-time favorites. The final dance scene always makes my heart flutter.

Damon doesn't text, so I contact him once I'm ready for bed.

Hey, sexy, what are you doing? I missed you tonight. I wish you were here. I'm climbing in bed to read Bound and thinking of you.

All my love,
Katarina

I expect to get a return text right away, but I don't. Twenty minutes later, Em knocks on my door.

"Come in."

The door opens, but it's not Em who enters. It's Damon, and he moves lightning fast toward me.

"I can't do it. I don't want to suffocate you, but I want to be with you every chance I can." He sits on the bed. "I got your text and drove right over. You said you wished I was here. I'm here."

"I'm glad. Climb in bed. It's late, and we have work tomorrow." I yawn before saying, "Before I forget. Should I worry about this Mara girl?"

"No. She's my past. You're my future."

TREVOR and I are swamped with menus, accommodations, transportation services, and invitations. These things are like time vampires and suck you dry.

I race to Damon's office at five, ready to discuss book club and pick out a slip of paper from our naughty bag. Did he write the same things as I did? It wouldn't surprise me. The longer I'm with him, the more I realize how alike we are.

"Are you ready to go?" I ask, skipping into his office.

"Yes. Let's grab a pizza on our way and eat in your bed?"

"Pizza in bed?" It's not our norm, but variety is good. "I can do that. We also need a bottle of wine because I'm celebrating. Tomorrow is my last day of school."

"We have lots to celebrate, like school ending, your graduation, book club, the opening of Ahz, and our relationship. Life is good, Katarina."

We pull up to my curb less than an hour later with a large pizza and a bottle of merlot.

Inside Damon's coat pocket is the naughty bag.

"I want to pick the first time," I say. "You can pick next week, and if this turns out to be too much fun, we'll pick more often." The thrill of the unknown ripples over my skin like fire.

"Okay." He opens the trunk and pulls out a plain brown box.

"What's that?"

"Some of my suggestions need props. I ordered items that may come up."

"Now you've piqued my curiosity. Should we skip the pizza and dig right into book club?" I race to the door, unlock it, and beat him to the bedroom.

"Not a chance." He closes the door behind him. Setting the pizza on my dresser, he flips it open. "You'll need sustenance. Eat first and read later. To prove I'm flexible, you can choose your poison before you eat."

He holds up the bag, and I reach inside and grab a scrap of paper. Written on it is the word: Bondage. I crumple it and throw it away.

"Hey, you can't throw away the ones you don't like. That's not fair."

"It said bondage. We've done that already. I want to try something new." I reach in for another and pull out a note that says, 'Watch Katarina pleasure herself.'

"Oh, my God, Damon, really?" I toss the paper at him and give him a suspicious look.

"I'm so excited you got that one. The odds were in my favor since I wrote it over twenty times."

"You cheated!" He tipped the scales to his side. Damon is a man that always gets what he wants.

"You didn't outline any rules. You said to write the things I found intriguing in the book. The subject was discussed, and it's at the top of my list. You also didn't put a limit to the number of times we could write something down."

"Fine." I strip down naked and sit cross-legged with the pizza box open and lying against my chest, but each time I close it, I give him a peek of what's coming.

"Do you want a slice? It's hot and steamy and waiting for you," I tease.

"What are you doing?" He reaches into the box to get a piece.

"I'm having fun. You wanted to watch, right? What's in the brown box? Anything I should use?" I pick the toppings off one slice and move the pizza box to my dresser.

I open the brown box and find everything under the sun inside it. The items range from handcuffs to vibrators. Reaching in, I grab exactly what I need to make my man's fantasy come true.

I HONESTLY DIDN'T THINK I could do it, but when I looked into his eyes and saw the anticipation, I couldn't let him down. As I come down from my high, I snuggle and ask, "Was it everything you thought it would be?"

I'm embarrassed in the aftermath. It was bold and wanton, but Damon makes me do things I never considered before.

"It was more."

We settle into bed and talk about the book.

"What did you think about this week's chapters? What about the scene with the beads?" I didn't think people used things like that.

"Nothing shocks me more than what you did for me just now. It shows if someone cares for you enough, they'll go out on a limb. I thought for sure you'd flat-out deny my request."

"I thought so too, but I couldn't refuse you when it would cost me so little. Love has a strange way of giving you courage."

"Thank you for leaving your comfort zone."

"I left my comfort zone the day I met you."

He undresses and climbs under the covers with me.

By the time I wake the next morning, Damon is showered and

dressed. He sits on the edge of the bed with a bag of pastries in his hand and a cup of steaming coffee placed next to my bed.

"Time to get up. It's your last day of classes, and I have to get to work." Leaning over to kiss me, he says, "Let's go out to dinner tonight to celebrate." He holds up the bag. "I bought you a cheese Danish. You once told me it was the way to your heart."

I stare at his gorgeous face and know I love him way too much. "A cheese Danish? You're pulling out all the stops." I peek inside. "You had my heart before the Danish." I smile at him. "The question is, how do I get to your heart?"

He leans over and kisses me once more before he dashes out the door. He's a master at deflection. It wasn't long ago that he told me he had no heart. There's no doubt he has one, but it's a shame he's protecting it like Fort Knox.

I TURN my term paper in and close my student accounts. It feels weird knowing I won't have another homework assignment. I don't have to walk onto this campus again for anything other than graduation.

Giddiness and sadness fill me in equal measure. Everyone moves on with their lives.

If I don't get a going, I'll be late. Taking the morning off already put me behind.

Trevor waits in the lobby with arms crossed. This isn't normal behavior. "What's wrong?" I look at his face for a hint, but there's nothing.

"Follow me to Della's office. She has paperwork for you to sign." He hurries to the elevator. "If you haven't had lunch, I'd like to take you."

I have several things planned for my afternoon—having a meeting with Della and lunch with Trevor was not on the list.

I follow him to the fifth floor, where he basically pushes me into Della Fields' office.

She grins as we enter, and she slides her paperwork aside. "Can I get you something to drink, Ms. Cross?"

Something is going on that makes my insides knot. Who gets called into the Human Resources Director's office without warning if it's not bad?

"Why am I here?" There's a quiver to my voice. "Did I do something wrong?"

Trevor remains silent.

"No. So far, you have done everything right," Ms. Fields says to my relief. "Trevor tells us you've become quite an asset to Noble Enterprises. Good people are hard to find, Ms. Cross. I understand you graduate on Monday."

"Yes."

"Zenith has grown exponentially, and now that we're co-branding with Anthony Haywood's, we expect to double in size over the next few years. We need good people to help us get to where we want to be."

I see her mouth is moving, but nothing makes sense. Why is she talking to me—an intern—about growth and development? And then I realize. She's offering me a job.

"I'm glad you're pleased with my contribution. Why am I here?" I tuck my hands behind my back and cross my fingers.

"We'd like to offer you a permanent position at Noble Enterprises. It's lower level, but I expect rapid promotions. The position would be a permanent assistant to Trevor." She looks in his direction, and they smile at each other. "You'd have your own office, although he would like you to spend a lot of your time overseeing Ahz. Even though we are co-branding with Anthony Haywood's, Zenith will manage the facility. Therefore, everything but the kitchen falls on our shoulders. What do you say?"

I look at Trevor, then at Della. Who gets offered a job like this straight out of college? *I do.* I swell with pride, so much so that I'm sure I've grown several inches.

"This is where I exit," Trevor says. "Thanks for letting me sit in, Della. The shock on her face was priceless." He chuckles all the way out the door.

"Ms. Cross, these are the specifics concerning the job offer." She hands me a job description that includes my beginning salary. Yes, salary—not an hourly wage, but a mid-level five-figure income.

"Please call me Katarina."

"Only if you call me Della. Take whatever time you need to think about it."

I glance down at the proposal and back up to Della. It's a great offer, but I need to know if I earned this on my own. "I have one question. Does Mr. Noble have anything to do with the hiring process here?"

She shakes her head. "He gets involved with upper-level management like directors. I handle all other hires." She chuckles. "Could you imagine trying to sit in on every interview or promotion? We have thousands of employees worldwide." She tilts her head. "Is there a reason you ask?"

"I know Mr. Noble and his family and want to make sure I earned this position."

"I can assure you, he doesn't know I offered you a job. Do you need to think about it overnight?"

"No, I love it here. I'll take the position. Where do I sign?"

The paperwork is painless, but it takes a long time to review. I sign a few non-disclosure agreements—one for Zenith, and one for Ahz. I initial my job proposal and new salary, and then Della explains benefits and company policy. After several hours, she shakes my hand and sends me on my way.

It's one thirty, and I've missed my lunch date with Damon. I pull out my phone and see one text message, one voicemail message, and an email.

Lunch is getting cold.
Did you get caught up somewhere?
I'm worried.
Damon

The email was more detailed.

From: Damon Noble

To: Katarina Cross

Subject: Where are you?

Where are you? Lunch has come and gone, and I've been waiting for you. It's not like you to not text or call. I'm worried. Call me as soon as you see this message.

Yours,

Damon

I get ready to listen to his voicemail when my phone rings. It's him.

"Hi! I'm so sorry. I got caught up with something and couldn't contact you."

"Thank goodness. I was worried about you. I thought maybe you had an accident. I kept thinking of that horrific crash we saw on the way to your parents' house. My heart's been in my stomach since you missed lunch."

"I'm okay, and I didn't mean to worry you. What's your schedule like this afternoon? I want to show you the gift bags, and I have news to share with you, but right now, I need to meet with Trevor."

"I'll free up time for you. My schedule is clear after four, but you can come in whenever you want." He lets out a breath. "I'm so relieved you're okay. Please, never do that again."

"I'm glad to hear your heart dropped into the bottom of your stomach. It proves you have one. See you later." I giggle as I hang up.

Trevor and I end up at the same hamburger joint we went to the day Damon saw me in the elevator. That was the day he learned I was interning at his company. It's kind of ironic because later, I'll tell him I work for him permanently.

AT FOUR O'CLOCK, I walk into Damon's office carrying one of the large leather bags. Sitting on top is the crowning glory of my accomplishment—a copy of *Bound* tied with a red silk scarf. He rises from his chair and takes the bag from my hands, placing it on his desk.

"This looks amazing. You haven't added an invitation to the book club, have you?" he teases.

"No, book club is by invite only, and I'm not interested in opening it to others."

"I'm relieved, I wouldn't be open to sharing either." His lips brush my cheek. "What kept you today? I ate both bowls of wonton soup and egg rolls waiting for you."

"What a sacrifice that must have been," I tug at my jacket. "I received a job offer and was negotiating my package."

His expression goes from wry to wary. He's definitely not happy about the job, but I left out the fact that it's here. It was my way of confirming he didn't know about the offer.

"You took a job?" The light in his eyes dim.

"Yes. It's a great company. They have fantastic benefits, and the pay is good. The best perk is that I'll be able to hook up with the president at lunch."

His face goes from confusion to realization.

"You got a job here?" The light is back. His eyes sparkle like gemstones in the sun. "I'm not surprised. You're a capable woman. What position did you get?"

"I'm Trevor's assistant."

"Hmm. That man gets to see you more than I do. Is it wrong for me to feel jealous?"

"That man would rather see you than me. He has specific tastes, and you're right up his alley."

"I never guessed, but hearing that makes him the perfect man for you to work with."

The changes in Damon's demeanor make me dizzy. I see concern, happiness, wickedness, anger, and now elation. I love elation the best.

CHAPTER TWENTY-FOUR

"Katarina Cross," the chancellor calls, and the roar of my fan club is deafening. Who would have thought I'd have so many people attending my graduation? The same roar happens when Emma climbs the stairs to receive her diploma.

We gather after the ceremony to take obligatory pictures.

My parents beam with pride as they hug me. We rotate through the group, making sure everyone gets their picture taken with the graduates. This will be the first picture Damon and I take together.

Damon's mom surprises me with her attendance, but she doesn't stay long because she has patients to attend to. Instead, we agree to meet for dinner the next night. Damon's not invited because Rose wants me all to herself, and that makes him uncomfortable and unhappy.

As the crowd dies down, we go to Anthony Haywood's to celebrate. Anthony set up a private room in the back for us.

He makes the day special for Emma. Seeing them together, warms my heart. They're in love, and Anthony makes no secret of it when he pulls her into his arms and tells her.

I stand to the side and watch them bask in love's glow. It occurs to me Damon may never say those three words I long to hear.

Can I be in a relationship where I'll never hear him say, I love you?

I can't imagine it. My life is centered around love. Love of family. Love of friends.

"A penny for your thoughts," Damon says. "You look troubled."

I glance at Emma and sigh.

"They look happy and in love, don't they?"

"I know little about love, but they do look happy and content."

I face him. "Do you think happy and content are enough? Is that what you want in your life? Are you okay with just being content?"

"Is content a bad thing?" His forehead furrows. "I thought you were happy?"

"I am happy, for now." My heart sinks. It won't be okay forever.

We stay through dinner and dessert and the opening of presents. Even I have gifts.

Rose gave me a day at the spa. My parents gave me a check for five thousand dollars and said it was left over from the college fund they'd set up when I was a kid. Trevor gave me a hard time, but he brought flowers and a card.

"I'm tired, can you take me home?"

Damon studies me but nods and walks me to his car.

Back home, I change and climb into bed.

The day exhausted me, and my emotions ran the gamut: There was relief that I graduated. Joy at seeing my family. Jealousy as my best friend stared lovingly into her man's eyes. Finally, shock when my brother sidled up to Trevor.

I sink into my pillow, happy to be in Damon's arms. He reaches over to grab something from the floor.

"I have a gift for you, too. It's personal, and I wanted to give it to you in private." In his hand is a blue velvet box.

I open it and find a beautiful and delicate necklace. Hanging from the thin chain is a gold angel wing. On the back is a tiny engraving that says, 'Forever Mine.'

The sentimental gift touches me because it took thought and planning.

I hug him and tell him I love him.

The only sound I hear is the beating of his heart and the slowing of his breath as he falls asleep, content in my arms.

CHAPTER TWENTY-FIVE

Tuesday begins with a bang—literally. I startle awake by a crash in the kitchen. I race to see what fell and find Damon barefoot, standing in a puddle of milk.

"What happened?"

"I tried to bring you coffee, and I dropped the milk. I made such a mess, but I'll clean it up while you shower."

"Nonsense. I'll help you."

"Now you sound like my mother," he scoffs. "Nonsense is one of her favorite words. She uses it to get her way. If you were to say you like whipped topping with your pie, she'd say, 'Nonsense. It tastes better with ice cream,' and you'd enjoy the ice cream just as much." He cups my cheeks and stares into my eyes. "Be careful with her tonight. She'll nonsense you where she wants you."

I laugh at his description of his mother. "Thanks for the warning. Should I come over after dinner?"

"I'll wait for you. What about lunch today?" He looks like a small boy asking for candy.

"I'll be there. Should I arrange for lunch?"

"Do you want to break Greta's heart? She takes it upon herself to make sure we're well-fed."

I help clean up the milk, and we head to the shower together. There is no sense in wasting water.

TREVOR GREETS me at my cubicle, and I notice my things are gone. He's so excited to show me to my new office, which is small, but mine.

On the door is a placard with my name, and below are the words Assistant Event Planner. During the last few months, my life changed from what I planned. It's amazing how a favor, a man, and a book turned my life upside down.

"It's not as big as your boyfriend's upstairs, but it's a good-sized office."

Feeling playful, I respond, "Nobody has one as big as my boyfriend's." I smile and give him a little punch in the arm.

"Since we're talking about men, tell me about your brother. We talked at your party last night, but all I know is he's cute and a banker?"

"Are you trying to pick up my brother?" I fist my hips. "First, it's my boyfriend, and now it's my brother," I tease. "You should meet up with him for lunch sometime. You could get to know each other and see if something comes of it. I saw you checking each other out last night."

"He checked me out?" A grin lifts the corners of his mouth. "I didn't notice."

"You're as subtle as a brick to the head, now get out of my office. I have work to do." He doesn't leave my office immediately.

"Give me your brother's number, and I'll leave you alone for the rest of the day."

I rattle off Chris's number and start organizing my new desk. The thing that would make it perfect is a picture of Damon.

With daily lunches, I no longer wait for Greta to announce my arrival. We're past the formal stage.

Greta knows better than anyone what goes on in that office, and to show her how much I appreciate her, I had flowers delivered this morning. She goes above and beyond the call of duty for both of us.

"Katarina, the flowers are beautiful, and congratulations on your graduation and new job."

"Thanks, Greta. It's been quite a week." I glance at the closed door. "Is he busy?"

"He's never too busy for you. Just head on in. I'm sure whatever he's doing will end once he sees you."

She's right. As soon as I enter the door, he tells whoever he's talking to that he needs to get back with them later.

"Hi, Angel. How's your day going?" He walks over and gives me a kiss before he reaches down to play with the angel wing necklace. His hand lingers just above my breast, causing my breath to hitch and my heart to race. "Tell me about your new office." His hands glide across my chest while his lips leave butterfly kisses across my neck.

"You make talking hard."

"You make me hard." He steps back, putting several feet between us. It's the only way we'll get through lunch clothed.

With only a couple of weeks left until the grand opening, things are moving at supersonic speed. Contracts and memos cover Damon's desk. He shuffles things around, picks up an envelope, and holds it in the air.

"This is your brother's personal invite. Let me know if you want to invite anyone else. I'm happy to accommodate any wish you have."

"Ah ... that is so sweet. Did you see my brother and Trevor? I'm not sure I want my boss and Chris dating. I mean, Trevor also wants to meet the drummer from the band, Rylan. Not only that, he wants me to help him pick out an outfit so he can turn heads. But I refuse to set him up with anyone if he's chasing after my brother."

"It will all work out the way it's supposed to, now tell me about your office."

"It's almost perfect. All it needs is a picture of you. Would you mind?"

"I don't mind, but people might wonder why you have my picture on your desk. Those who don't know we're dating might find it odd."

I think about it for a moment and realize he's got a point. Workplace romances should be kept out of the workplace. I'll settle for a picture of him next to my bed.

I SHOW up early to dinner with Rose and get us a table at the Greek restaurant she picked out.

"Sorry I'm late, Katarina. I had a tough case today. It's heartbreaking when you have to tell a parent their child is terminal, and they have little time." She flags the waiter over and orders a glass of wine.

"I'm so sorry. It would be hard under any circumstances, but given that you've been through it yourself, I bet it's near impossible."

Rose takes the wine before it hits the table. "It's never easy, but since I've lived through it, I have a great deal of empathy." She drinks and exhales the stress of her day. "I know what they're feeling because I've done it twice. Simon passed away when the boys were twelve and fourteen. It was a difficult time. Roman passed eight years later."

"Damon told me about Simon. He has fond memories of his father." Remembering the tree house and carved letters, I tell her about visiting their old home. "He took me to the tree house they built a few weeks ago."

Rose's eyes soften. "I'm glad he's sharing things with someone. You're good for him."

"He's good for me too."

"He cares for you, Katarina. I can see it in his eyes. I haven't seen him look at anyone that way since Mara."

The mention of Mara throws me off balance. I sip my wine and collect my thoughts. "I don't know much about Mara, but I walked into his office one day while he argued with her on the phone."

Rose stays silent for several minutes. "I don't know what happened between them. Everything seemed to fall apart at once." She sighs. "His brother got sick, his relationship broke apart ... it was too much for him to handle, I guess. He's never been the same since." Her brow furrows. "I'm surprised he's talking to Mara again."

"I think it was just the one phone call, but I don't know." Looking down at the table, I ask, "Was Roman sick for a long time? Watching someone you love fade away has to be hard."

"No, it came as a shock to us. We didn't know he was sick. One day he came down with flu-like symptoms, and a month later, he died." She purses her lips. "Roman and Damon struggled with their relationship before Roman got sick. I don't think they reconciled, and Damon carries that burden with him."

Rose and I talk during dinner. She tells me how she wants to take me to the Getty Museum to see the impressionist exhibition. That she loves visiting wineries throughout California and has a large collection in her cellar. Also, she discusses how she works too much and plays too little. But mostly, we talk about Damon.

"I'm glad we had this time to ourselves. Damon is a good man, Katarina. With you, he is less serious, he smiles more, and he laughs more. I like what I see when he's with you."

"Thanks, Rose. I love your son, but I'm not sure he's capable of returning that love."

Rose scrunches her lips, then shakes her head. "Nonsense. Everyone is capable of love. Damon was always a loving boy. You need to figure out how to break into his heart. Honestly, I think you already did, but he's not ready to admit it."

Rose and I part ways with a promise to visit the Getty soon. Thirty minutes later, I reach Damon's house and key in 0615 to open the gate.

He materializes in the doorway as I drive forward.

"Hey, sexy man. I brought you a little Greek for dinner," I say when I get out of the car. "Are you interested?"

"Is her name Katarina?"

I lift the to-go container. "I brought you lamb kabobs and Greek salad with a side of me. Will that do?"

"I suppose it'll have to." He meets me on the porch. "How was dinner with my mother?"

"It was nice. We're going to the Getty sometime soon, and she wants to teach me about wine collecting."

I take his hand and pull him into the kitchen to transfer his food to a real plate.

"Did she nonsense you to death?" He spears a piece of lamb.

"No, she only said it once, and it was during a benign part of our conversation."

"I missed you."

"I missed you, too. What did you do the last two hours?"

"I hit the gym, then came home and read the final pages of our book to prepare for book club tomorrow night. Do you want book club here or at your house? Our schedule is mixed up."

"I'm flexible. Whatever you want is fine with me."

"Tell you what. Let's pull a note from the naughty bag and decide then. If we need something from the brown box, then we go to your house."

"Okay." I agree easily. "It's your turn to pick. Where's the bag?"

"It's in my jacket pocket in the bedroom." He drops his fork. "I'll race you."

He shoots past me, leaving his half-eaten dinner behind. I'm right on his tail and almost overtake him on the landing, but his arms wrap around my middle, impeding my progress.

We enter the room laughing.

I throw myself on the big comfy bed and wait for him to retrieve the bag. He plops on the bed next to me and hands it over. I make him close his eyes so he can't see what he's selecting and have him reach in and pull out one folded piece of paper.

"What's it say?" I ask excitedly.

His eyes light up. "Oh, this is good. It's another one of my notes."

I look at him suspiciously and take the note from his hand. It says Griffith Park Observatory.

"What does this mean? I don't recall any part of the book taking place there."

"We talked about this. Since the book isn't set in California, I took creative license to substitute, and I chose Griffith Park Observatory."

"Hmm, sex in public again. What if we get caught?"

"We won't get caught because I'll protect you. Wear that cute little blue miniskirt and those sexy black heels." He stares at the tenting of his pants. "Look what you do to me." He adjusts himself. "Are you game, Katarina?"

I'm silent because it rocks Damon's cocky confidence. When he's vulnerable, things turn out better. In the end, he'll win because his sexy self-assurance is a total turn-on for me.

"Can I let you know tomorrow?" His lower lip pops out in a pout. I take my index finger and pluck at it. "I need to think on it overnight. You'll know my answer tomorrow."

His expressive eyes look at me with hope.

"Can we talk about the book?"

"I swear there's exhibitionism. I wouldn't lie to you."

"I'm sure there is, but that's got nothing to do with my question. We're getting to the end of the book, and I wonder where their relationship is going. His issues have molded him from childhood to the present. Do you think they can make it work? Can someone put the pains of their past behind them to have a future? I mean, how much is too much?"

And there it is—a look of sheer terror clouds his eyes. The question is about more than the book, it's about us, and he knows it. *Bound* mirrors many things in our relationship. The favor, the connection, the need, the insecurity, the chemistry, and the conflict —it's all there. Change the storyline just a little, and it could be about us.

"Since I finished the book, I know how their story ends, but I don't think you're asking me about them, are you?"

"I am," I begin, "but I'm also asking you if I'll always have to settle for happy and content."

He takes a long breath and releases a longer exhale. "I want happy and content, but I also want you to feel loved." He takes my hands. His expression is earnest. "Do you feel loved?"

"I feel confused. Everything you do and say makes me feel loved and cherished, yet you can't utter the words."

"I'm trying. I am. Be patient with me while I work things out in my head. My heart belongs to you. You know that."

I nod in resignation. "I feel your love, but someday I want the words. There's a disconnect between your heart and your head." Just like in the book, I wonder how it will end for us. Will we get our happily ever after, or do I settle for less than I need? Those are my last thoughts before I fall asleep, curled next to his body.

CHAPTER TWENTY-SIX

"What are your intentions concerning my brother, Trevor?" Feeling vulnerable in my relationship, I want to make sure Chris won't end up in the same boat. Loving someone emotionally unavailable is heartbreaking.

"My intentions are to have lunch with him today and see where that takes us. I haven't bought the engagement ring yet if that's what you're asking."

"I don't want Chris to get hurt. You jumped all over the chance to meet the drummer of Reluctant Capitalists. Don't lead my brother on. If you like him, then great, but if you plan to toy with him, quit now."

"Kat has her claws out. What's going on? Bad night?"

This has nothing to do with my night, and everything to do with taking care of my family. "No, I'm protecting what belongs to me. I don't want you pursuing my brother if you're chasing Rylan."

"I get you a job, and now you think you rule the world," he jokes. "Give me more credit than that. I'd love to meet the drummer because he's hot, but I'm a realist. Do you think I'd be anything more than a quickie for him? I told you, I'm looking for the one. Not the one-night stand."

I hug him. He's a good guy, and I feel terrible thinking his motives were less than honorable.

"I'm sorry I doubted you. So much has happened in such a small amount of time, and I'm trying to wrap my brain around everything." I pull the invitation Damon gave me out of my bag and offer it to him. "When you see Chris today, will you give him this invitation to the grand opening?" I touch his arm. "Have a great lunch and tell him hello for me. He likes sweet tea. Just a hint in case you get there earlier than he does."

LUNCH WITH DAMON GOES WELL. We relax and fill the time with conversation and laughter. He regales me with stories of other openings. It's amazing what people will do or wear. His funniest story is about a guest who wore assless chaps. After several drinks, the man stumbled and fell against the buffet table, where his bare flesh came in contact with a lit Sterno can. Zenith no longer uses open flames.

The man sued Noble Enterprises, but the judge threw the case out when he found out the man knowingly dressed in bottomless pants.

I laughed so hard when he told me the judge's words to the plaintiff as he walked out of the courtroom were, "Watch your back ... end."

"I'm leaving early today," I tell Damon after lunch. "I'm cooking dinner for us tonight and need to stop by the grocery store. Do you mind if I go into your house without you there?"

"You practically live there. I'll have a key made for you." He takes his house key from his ring and hands it to me. "Use this for now. I'll stop by the hardware store and have one made." He hems and haws. "Did you decide about tonight?"

"No, I'm considering your request and will let you know when you get home." After a quick peck on his lips, I rush for the door. "Got to run. Need to stop at Ahz and make sure things are on track. See you tonight."

Driving in downtown in Los Angeles is like entering a war zone. No one wants to be on the roads between six and ten in the morning or any time after two in the afternoon.

The freeways are death traps, and the seven-mile trip takes forty-five minutes. Thank God for parking privileges. If I had to hunt down a parking space, I'd waste another thirty minutes.

I enter and find most of the construction workers gone. Only a handful of people remain to take care of last-minute details.

The VIP lounge is ready for the elite list of guests attending. It's strictly A-listers, ranging from professional athletes to movie stars and politicians. Inviting only one hundred VIPs and their guests is smart. There wouldn't be enough room for more egos.

Once I'm comfortable with the preparations and the storage of the gift bags, I leave to prepare dinner and change into a miniskirt and heels.

IT'S strange to be in his house by myself. Though I've become familiar with it since I spend half of each week here, it's empty without him.

The baked chicken, quinoa, and steamed spinach are ready, and I'm dressed in the outfit he requested.

The alarm system alerts me to the gate being opened. *So that's how he knows when I'm here.*

Like him, I walk to the front entry and watch him drive forward.

A big grin takes over his face when he sees me dressed in my blue mini.

Throwing the Mustang into park, he jumps out and races to me. His arms are a vise around my waist and hold me tightly while he twirls us in circles. I never thought an outfit could bring a person such joy.

"Are you hungry?" I ask.

He kisses my neck, giving me a gentle bite where my shoulder and neck meet. "Ravenous."

My conversation centers on food, but he has Griffith Park on his mind.

"Food first. You can satisfy your other hunger later." I grab him by the tie and pull him into the kitchen.

I prepare our dishes while Damon races upstairs to change. He returns wearing black jeans and a snug-fitting designer T-shirt, and Lord, he looks amazing. On his feet are a beautiful pair of leather loafers, and his D & G cologne fills the air. In his hand is a trench coat.

I take the coat and set it aside before leading him to the breakfast bar where we enjoy our dinner and talk about the day.

"How are things at the club?" he asks. "I don't know if I'll ever be able to sit in the VIP lounge and not think of you on the floor above me. Out of all my clubs, Ahz is my favorite because of you. I love that we're both invested in its success."

"I love that, too. I think the VIP lounge will be the death of me though. I'm on a huge learning curve, and I'm just reaching the top of the arc."

"I met with Trevor yesterday, and he said he let go of the reins and had you take charge. He would never allow you to run a big project if he didn't think you could handle it."

"He's a great boss and a good friend."

Damon pushes his empty plate away.

"Shall we go? The observatory is best if it's seen as day turns from dusk to dark. It's my favorite place to think."

"Let me wash the dishes, and then we'll leave."

He grabs my arm and takes me directly to the Mustang. "I pay Claire a healthy salary to clean this house. She can do the dishes tomorrow morning when she gets here." He opens the door and helps me inside. "By the way, dinner was great. I haven't come home to a cooked meal since I left my mom's house." He kisses me and rounds the car to climb behind the steering wheel.

"I like to cook." I turn to him. "We eat out too much, and I'm gaining weight. Outside of making love, I don't get any exercise. You're bad for my health."

"I told you I was bad for you. You were warned."

WITH MULTIPLE OBSERVATION platforms at Griffith Park, we see the surrounding area from different vantage points. It's impossible to locate a more secluded space to see the city or star gaze.

Damon knows exactly where he wants to go and walks me to the highest point. I've been turned on since we got into the car. I know it's crazy, but I like what he likes. I get worked up over the thrill of the unknown and unexpected. This is a new world for me.

He picks a place where no one is near and takes the long coat from his shoulders and pulls it to cover mine, creating a tent that surrounds us.

His lips are on my neck and his breath near my ear. Desperate hands slide around my waist and raise to cup my breasts.

"Lean against me, Angel. Relax and enjoy." I love those words. 'Relax and enjoy' means 'Hang on for dear life because I'll go somewhere you've never been.'

I melt into his chest and let him control my body. His cologne is intoxicating to smell. Watching the setting sun paint the sky in reds and oranges pleases my eyes. His touch ignites a fire inside me. His voice whispers the things every girl wants to hear. Things like, "You're beautiful. You make me happy, and I've always wanted to do this." The only sense not activated is taste. Eventually, he'll kiss me, and I'll taste the sweetness of his lips against mine.

Damon gets bolder. His hands travel to my skirt and pull it to my waist. As he reaches down, he gasps because I'm not wearing underwear.

"You always surprise me. When did you decide to do this?"

I answer in short, breathless answers. "The observatory or the underwear?" There's no thinking with his hands on me.

To the passerby, we look like we're enjoying the sunset. Many men wrap their coats around their girlfriends when the sun sets, and the air turns chilly. The only difference is his fingers are deep inside me, and he's whispering sexy things in my ear.

"Both."

I lean back and let him support my weight.

"Yesterday."

He drives me crazy, and when the pad of his thumb rubs against my bundle of nerves, I fall over the edge.

He continues to whisper. "That's right. Let it roll over you. I've got you. Breathe and enjoy, because in just a minute, I'll be inside you, and when you want to scream ... kiss me. Do you understand?"

I answer with a nod.

He turns me around and sits me on the edge of the wall. The rough cement scrapes against my ass when he scoots me to the edge and impales me. My breath hitches at the shock of it. How he got himself out of his pants and into me is nothing short of magic.

The jacket tents around us, only this time, I face him with my legs wrapped around his waist as he repeatedly plunges inside me. The heat builds, and I push my lips to his and let my muffled scream escape into his mouth.

The power of his thrusts, the excitement of making love in the open, and the friction of the cement take me to the top, and he follows me off the edge. Our lips stay fused while we swallow each other's passion.

"It's such a lovely place, isn't it?" a voice asks from our right side.

He pulls me closer, pushing himself deeper. My eyes pop wide as we look at the stranger next to us.

The old man seems harmless, but it's an odd sensation to talk to a stranger while my boyfriend is deep inside me. We let our guard down at the peak of our passion, and now we're stuck until he leaves.

"It's my favorite place in the world." Damon looks at me with a mischievous smile.

Thankfully, the old man realizes we'd rather be alone and turns to leave. He chuckles as he walks away.

Within seconds, Damon tucks himself back into his pants, and I'm back on two feet with my skirt pulled down. He takes the coat off and wraps it around my shoulders.

He said he'd protect me, and he did. I felt safe in his arms.

"I'd take you to the planetarium and pleasure you under the dome, but we've had enough for tonight. What do you think?" he asks.

He leans down, sweeps me off my feet, and carries me all the way to the car.

"Which is it? Griffith Park, or the restaurant?" I ask.

"What about them?" he asks.

"Where is your favorite place?"

"My favorite place is wherever you are."

He says things that have a way of stealing my heart. "My favorite place is wherever you are, too. Every time we make love, it's my favorite time. Every kiss you give me is my favorite kiss. I'd have never guessed I'd be in this place three months ago."

"It's funny how life works, isn't it? Let's go home and finish the book," he says.

"Do you think we could pick another book after the grand opening?" I don't want to give this part of our lives up. It's the one time I can ask questions.

"Yes, but can we still grab from the naughty bag? There are way too many notes to overlook."

As soon as we arrive at his house, I run for the shower while he makes us hot chocolate. We snuggle up with each other and begin our final discussion about *Bound*.

"Okay, so they ended up together, which is nice, but do you think they'll be happy?" I ask, starting our book club discussion.

"I don't know. Is anyone ever completely happy? There's no perfect relationship. Being with someone takes a certain amount of compromise. There was a lot of discussion on their part about limits, and I think being honest about your limits is crucial."

"I read the last chapter twice. He destroyed that contract, which meant he wanted to move forward. That she was willing to keep it meant she'd accepted their relationship for what it was. I'm happy they figured out something that worked for them."

"It was all about negotiation," he says.

"What if you don't know what you're willing to compromise on?"

"Are we talking about the book or us?"

"I suppose I'm talking about us. I'm sorry, let me ask something else."

"It's okay. You can ask me anything. Honestly, I'm surprised you haven't asked more questions. My answer would be, only *you* can decide what's good for you or not good for you. Why don't you ask more questions?"

"You've met my parents. They're inquisitive and intrusive. Some things are better left alone. Some things aren't anybody's business." I snuggle against him. "I have lots of questions, but you come across as someone who doesn't like to share. That's why I don't ask."

"I don't have dark secrets, just painful memories." He looks down at his hands as he nervously twists the lower part of his T-shirt around his fingers.

"Hopefully, someday you'll trust me enough to share your pain." I don't look at him because I don't want him to see my eyes. To see the need I have for him to talk to me.

"What do you know of pain?" He asks with a hint of sarcasm.

"More than you'd think. Do you think you can come out unscathed when your best friend climbs into your arms to cry over the loss of her mother? What about when your brother gets beaten to a pulp for liking men instead of women? What about loving someone who can never love you back? I know pain, Damon. I feel yours every day, and it hurts me too."

He pulls away. "I'm sorry. I didn't consider Emma and Chris. You would feel the pain of the people you love." He pauses before continuing. "You want to know about Mara, so I'll tell you what I can." He runs his hand through his hair. "She was the first girl I ever loved. We dated for two years, and I foolishly thought she was the one. We lost our virginity together. We lived and breathed each other for so long, she became a part of me."

He inhales and closes his eyes.

"I emptied my soul into that relationship, and she destroyed me with one act of deception. I caught her with another man, and it gutted me." He moves so we can look into each other's eyes. "I haven't seen her since. I don't know why she called. Maybe she feels guilty. Maybe it's something else. It was ten years ago, and it still fills me with rage when I think about it."

"Thank you for sharing. It means more than you know."

CHAPTER TWENTY-SEVEN

The next two weeks pass by quickly, and the grand opening of Ahz is upon us.

Damon and I never discussed what he shared weeks ago. I think about his pain and how it would feel to have someone betray your trust in such a way. Sometimes I fantasize about running into Mara and kicking her ass.

"What are you wearing tonight?" I ask as he walks from the bed to the bathroom. He's a gorgeous man, solidly built and beautifully displayed.

"I'll wear a suit. Do you want to pick it out for me?" he asks.

"I love the suit you had on the day I came to your office to return your money. It's a blue pinstripe. That was the day you kissed me senseless and sent me on my way."

"That's the one I'll wear, then. What about you?"

"Definitely pants. I'm walking all over the club tonight, and I'm not showing my goodies to anybody."

"Anyone but me, right?" He raises a brow in amusement.

"We have an agreement. You're mine, and I'm yours."

"Never forget it." He dresses in the suit he wore the day we met.

"I'll be at the club all day, so I can't have lunch with you. When will you come over?" I ask.

He tightens the knot. "I'll make it before everything gets crazy."

It's disappointing I won't be able to see him at lunch today, but I know he has a busy schedule. There's a press conference in the afternoon and a ribbon-cutting ceremony at five. Then all hell breaks loose.

I change into navy blue leather pants and a silver button-down blouse Trevor helped me pick out but can't decide on which shoes to wear.

"Damon. Do you think I should wear the heels or the boots?"

He looks me up and down. His eyes turn a darker blue—a stormy I've-got-to-have-you-now blue. With one boot and one heel on, I turn in a circle so he can see them from every angle.

"I have a fondness for the heels. They bring back pleasant memories. I love those pants too; they hug your bottom like a second skin."

"Heels it is then, and I'm glad you love the pants. Trevor picked them out, but I bought them because I knew you'd like them."

"I'll like them better when I get to peel them off you tonight." He gives me another look and shakes his head before he walks out of the room and down the stairs.

Since we're going in different directions, we leave in separate cars. Trevor and I meet in the VIP lounge at eight this morning to go over everything for the night. We leave no stone unturned. The band accommodations are set. The greenroom amenities are in place. The Kogi people are scheduled to arrive at six. The band goes on at seven. I know everything is in order because I check it a dozen times, but it will be nice to have a second set of eyes to confirm.

Trevor seems relaxed and happy. "What's up with you?"

He smiles in his boyish way, then surprises me with his next statement. "Your brother dropped me off. He needed to be at work earlier than me."

My mouth hangs open. "You spent the night together?"

"Do you want the dirty details or the shortened version?"

I cringe at the thought of getting the down and dirty from Trevor. "Just give me a G-rated overview."

"You bailed on shopping day for me, and your brother said he'd come along. He has fabulous taste, don't you think?" Trevor stands and twirls in front of me in the same manner I did for Damon that morning.

"Who picked out the bow tie?"

"Chris chose the whole ensemble, from the pants to the sweater vest and bow tie."

"He did an excellent job. Do you have matching outfits?"

"No, but we compliment each other."

"I can't wait to see what he's wearing." A text comes in from Em telling me to break a leg.

My nerves twitch, and my hands shake. "Can you believe it's happening? The opening. The band. Do you still want to meet Rylan?"

"Chris and I want to meet the band together."

His statement pleases me, and I smile.

"What are you grinning about?" he asks.

"You really like my brother, and I'm excited about that. You're both great people. I think I'll like having you as my brother's boyfriend."

"One day at a time," he cautions with a smile. "How are things with lover boy?"

"Why do you call him lover boy?"

"I see when you come back from lunch. You always have that 'just laid' blush about you. I swear if I had sex that often, my dick would fall off."

"On that note, let's get to work."

We go through the guest list and identify everyone and their guests but two. Sam Wilson and Tory Blake have not called in the names of their dates, so we'll figure it out when they get here. It takes all morning and most of the afternoon to complete our checklist, but things are in order.

"Everything looks good, Katarina. I feel comfortable leaving everything in your capable hands. I've never enjoyed an opening, but that changes tonight. I have a date with a hot banker, and I plan to dance his ass off."

Trevor leaves the lounge with pep in his step. Thinking about how crazy the night will be, I lean my head against the booth and rest my eyes.

"There you are," Damon says. "I looked everywhere for you. Then I found Trevor, and he said he left you fifteen minutes ago. What are you doing?"

I rub my tired eyes. "How did the press conference go? I wish I could have seen it. Instead, I spent the day with Trevor, going over every detail. The night is just beginning, and I'm exhausted."

He climbs into the booth next to me and pulls me toward him, so my head rests on his shoulder.

"The press conference went well. It would have been better if you were there with me. Everything is better when we are together. And tonight, I feel like this is *our* grand opening."

We lean against the back of the velvet booth and kiss like teenagers. There are so much excitement and tension in the air, and Damon is my Valium. His presence relaxes me. It's funny how he can calm me and rouse at the same time.

"Come with me to let the masses in. I want you to stand beside me. Emma and Anthony will be there. It's a big night for all of us."

We walk hand in hand to the front doors of the lobby. Em stands with Anthony, looking beautiful in her purple cocktail dress. Anthony dressed to match her with a purple shirt and a black tie.

They stand on one side of the foyer, while Damon and I stand on the other. Everything is quiet until the bouncers open the doors, and the guests pour in.

I KISS Damon goodbye and tell him I'll find him later. I see Chris and Trevor near the elevator dressed in coordinating sweater vests and bow ties. All seems right with the world.

"Ready to meet the band?" I ask.

We maneuver down an employee hallway and catch the staff elevator to the second floor. I've learned every secret passageway throughout the building. I've spent enough time here, I can find my way blindfolded.

Trevor and Chris follow me into the greenroom, where the three of us wait for the band. In typical celebrity fashion, they show up with enough time to smack down several shots and eat some Kogi.

Chris and Trevor engage in conversation with all the band members, but they find common ground with the drummer. As they talk, Trevor slides his arm around Chris' waist. He's taking possession, and it warms my heart.

When the band hits the stage, I leave the greenroom to check out the rest of the club. The third-floor dance club is old school with music from the 80s and 90s. The energy is high, and everyone seems to have a good time.

The fourth floor is techno music. The pace here is more frantic, and instead of traditional dancing, jump-styling seems to be popular.

The sixth floor plays the current hits—top forty, along with popular indie bands. This is my favorite club. I glide across the floor to the sound of One Republic, keeping my eyes open for Damon when I see him through the glass floor below.

I race to the VIP lounge. It's packed with people—standing room only. I weave my way through the crowd to the other side.

As I approach, Damon is there with his arms caging a woman's shoulders. She's stunning with Mila Kunis eyes and a Kate Upton body. Her long, brunette hair hangs in loose curls around her shoulders. Her hand comes to his cheek. I can't hear anything, but I recognize the body language. She leans into him, and he does nothing. *Who the hell is this girl?*

As I venture forward, her hand slides to his neck, and she pulls him to her. Her ample breasts crush against his chest, and her lips capture his mouth. I'm paralyzed in place.

The scene unfolds in slow motion. He pushes her away. As soon as he turns, he sees me and stops dead. He stares at me like he's battling something inside. Eyes sad, body rigid, skin pale.

He glances back at the woman and then at me as if he's torn between us. When his eyes connect with mine, my life changes.

The kiss is forgivable, but the way he looks at her is unforgettable. I see the love I want and the suffering I hoped to erase from his life.

Glacier-blue eyes, filled with sorrow, stare back at me. They reflect the horrific memories of his troubled past. He moves toward me, the girl following on his heels.

"Katarina, it's not what you think!"

It's exactly what I think. I look past him to the woman standing next to him like that's her place.

I want to disappear into the floor, go back ten minutes, and skip the sixth floor. I want to fall to my knees and cry, but I'm not that girl. I'm Kat Cross and stronger than he'll ever know.

Shoring my shoulders, I step closer and reach out my hand to introduce myself. "Hi, I'm Kat, Damon's ex-girlfriend. You must be Mara." With nothing left to say, I turn and walk away.

Damon calls from behind me, but I am faster than he is or more forceful with the crowd. I exit through an employee entrance and move through the maze until I'm far away from Damon, Mara, and heartbreak.

My phone pings relentlessly with messages from Damon, but I ignore them.

By the time I make it to the greenroom, the band is gone, and I'm finally alone. The quiet is a blessing and a curse. It's nice to sit and take stock of my life, but awful to see where it's taken me.

This is not where I expected tonight to end. I was supposed to go home and make love to my man. The irony is, he was never mine. The minute I saw him look at her, I knew who she was, and who he belonged to. He would never be mine if he couldn't reconcile his past with her.

My hands shake, but I need to keep moving. There isn't time for a breakdown. When I get home, I'll let it all out, but for now, I need to focus on getting through the next few hours.

Tears fall, but I tip my head back, willing them to return to where they came from.

CHAPTER TWENTY-EIGHT

I approach my car and find Damon leaning against the door. My heart aches at the sight of him. Where there used to be love, now there is pain.

He was right. I knew nothing about it until tonight.

"Katarina, please talk to me. I've been trying to find you all night." His eyes plead, and his voice cracks.

"Damon, if you do nothing else for me in your life, step away from my car and leave me alone. I'm not ready to talk. I'm tired, hungry, and I want to be alone." I don't know where that strong voice came from, but the woman who spoke was fierce and meant business.

"Let me take you home and feed you. We can talk." He steps from the car and moves toward me.

My palm shoots out like a stop sign. "Stop. Don't touch me, don't talk, and don't call me. I'll contact you when I'm ready, not when you decide it's time. Now move out of the way so I can leave."

He steps back, and I get into my car, start the engine, and drive away.

In the rearview mirror, I see him standing in the center of the garage alone and as broken as I feel.

I make it home in record time and can't move fast enough toward the front door. I fumble with my keys as the tears fall. With Em staying at Anthony's tonight, I'll be alone in with my grief.

The bottle of wine Rose gave me weeks ago sits on the kitchen counter, and I can't think of a reason not to open it.

My phone beeps continuously as messages from Damon flood in. I glance at the screen and see his plea to let him know I got home safely.

"I'm safely home." I type back and turn off my phone. Over the next hour, I empty the bottle.

I wake up on the couch, still dressed in my leather pants and silver top. Subconsciously or consciously, I avoided climbing in bed. Sleeping there would remind me of the last time Damon and I were there, and I wasn't ready to deal with it then, but today is a new day.

Bracing myself for the emotional impact, I move to my room and take an inventory of my life.

On the dresser sits the flowers he sent the day after I met him. They dried so beautifully that I didn't have the heart to throw them away. Now they're a reminder of our relationship. Dead and lifeless.

In the corner of my room is the plain brown box full of possibilities I'll never experience. Opening my closet door, I come face-to-face with his section. Hanging neatly on the rack are a few of his suits, a pair of jeans, and several shirts. I hold the lapel of the black suit and bring it to my nose. The smell of him lingers in the fibers and permeates my soul. The only way to get him out of my life is to erase him from it.

I return to the kitchen to gather the supplies I need to expunge Damon Noble from my life, or at least my home.

Armed with a trash bag, I toss the flowers, pack up his clothes, and throw the brown box in the back corner of my closet.

I rip the sheets off my bed and toss them in the washer with double the soap. Satisfied, I strip myself and head to the shower. The hot water flows over my aching body and hides the tears I shed while I try to wash away his essence.

The ring of the house phone cuts my shower short. Fear stops me from answering it right away. It might be him, but by the third ring, I give in.

"Hello."

"Thank God! Where have you been?" It's Em, and she's frantic.

"I've been home. I turned my cell phone off last night and fell asleep. What's wrong?"

"I'll tell you what's wrong, Damon showed up this morning still wearing his suit from the opening and smelling of alcohol. All he said was that you left him, and then he passed out. What the hell is going on?"

"It's true. We're no longer together." I swallow the lump in my throat. "It's not something I can talk about right now or over the phone. I need to be there before the band goes on for round two. Will you be home tonight?"

"Kat, I'll come home right now if you need me." I know it's true. Em would drop everything for me.

"No, tonight is fine. I'll be home around eleven."

How I'll get through tonight is a mystery, but staying busy will keep my mind off Damon. It's not that I hate him. I could never hate someone I love, but loving him isn't enough.

THE CLUB IS BUSTLING, the band is happy, and the VIP lounge is taken care of. There are so many staff members seeing to the needs of our guests, it's wasteful. The payroll must be astronomical.

When I get home, I find Em waiting inside with several bottles of wine.

"Is this a light crying night that requires a chardonnay, or do we need to go for the heavy stuff like a merlot or a cabernet?" she asks.

"Let's go straight for the merlot. How many bottles did you bring?"

"After seeing Damon, I bought three bottles of everything."

"That should get us started," I try to joke, but break into sobs.

For the first time in over a decade, I trade places with Em. She cradles me against her bosom while I cry my eyes out. I sob until there are no tears left. We sit in silence until she asks me to explain.

"Mara happened." I tell her the story.

"Are you sure he kissed her? I just don't think Damon would do that."

"Are you siding with him?"

"No, but that just doesn't seem like Damon."

I sagged against the sofa back. "You're right, she kissed him. He didn't initiate it, and if I'm honest with myself, I don't even think he enjoyed it. He actually backed away." I finish my glass and pour another. "But it wasn't even the kiss that had me so upset; it was the look that sealed the deal. Do you remember when you told me if a man cautions you about himself, then you should listen to his warnings? Damon warned me again and again, and I didn't listen. He told me he didn't have a heart to give, and I didn't believe him. I was so convinced that I had a heart big enough for both of us. What was I thinking?"

Em holds me in her arms, where my tears had soaked her T-shirt.

"I'm so mad at him," she says. "It's taking everything in me to stay here and not go knee him in the balls."

I shake my head. "It's not his fault. It's mine. He was honest from the beginning. He told me he didn't date. He told me he couldn't offer me what I wanted or needed. He told me she'd gutted him, and she was the one, but I was so sure my love would be enough to overcome all of that. The only thing he said that wasn't true was that he wasn't a heartbreaker, always the heartbroken, but dammit, he broke mine."

The tears start up again and continue throughout the night until I wake up on the couch with a pillow under my head and a blanket over my body.

I stretch to get the kinks that have settled into my back ironed out.

"Today is the first day of the rest of my life." I climb off the couch and change into shorts, a T-shirt, and running shoes. "If it doesn't kill me, it will strengthen me."

CHAPTER TWENTY-NINE

The Mustang is missing when I arrive at work, and its absence comes as a relief.

Reaching into the back seat, I pick up the box of Damon's things and take them to the top floor.

Greta greets me like always.

"Hello, Katarina. How are you today?" She smiles. "I hear the opening was a smash. You must be so proud."

"It was a great opening, but a long weekend. Ahz was so well received by the press and the public that I'm sure it will continue to thrive."

"Mr. Noble looked handsome at the press conference. Did you see it?"

"No, I was busy with planning, but I love that suit on him." I think about Damon in his blue pinstripe suit, and my heart twists like a wet rag being rung dry. "Can you give these things to Mr. Noble when he gets in?"

She bends her head in question. She knows something is up, but as a professional, she doesn't ask questions.

She takes the clothes from my hand. "He called and said he wouldn't be in for a few days. Is there anything else you need? Anything I can do for you?"

"No, everything is okay." I offer her a weak smile and leave for my office.

A beautiful vase of flowers sits on my desk. The envelope says, "Angel" and I know they're from him. I collapse into my chair and stare at them.

Trevor enters my office and sits on the corner of my desk.

"Are you going to open the card, or do I have to do it?" he asks.

"I'll open it later."

"Hey, I know what's going on. Em called your brother, and he told me. Are you okay?" He hops up and walks behind my chair. His hands go straight to my shoulders to massage the stress away. "Do we need to kick his ass?"

"I knew what I was getting into. If anyone needs an ass-kicking, it's me. Damon is a good man, and I don't want people judging him over our breakup."

Trevor studies my face before leaving me alone.

I turn the envelope over and open it.

Katarina,

I never set out to hurt you. I adore you and can't imagine life without you in it. Please talk to me.

Damon

He thinks I left because of the kiss. Pulling out my phone, I send the hardest text of my life.

Damon,

Thank you for the flowers. I'm not ready to face this situation head-on. Give me time. Let's meet in a couple of weeks. How about Anthony Haywood's at Ahz on the third? I'll make the reservations. I hope you're okay.

Kat

My phone pings with an incoming message.

Kat, I'm relieved to hear from you. You don't understand how important you are. While I don't want to wait that long, I'll respect your wishes.

Yours,

Damon

I trace my finger over the word yours. Too bad that's not true; he was and never will be *mine*.

For the next few hours, Trevor and I plan, and when I return to my office at noon, I find Greta setting lunch on my desk.

"What are you doing?"

"I'm delivering your lunch. It's what I do." She gives me a don't-mess-with-me look and leaves.

I PULL into the garage today and see his parking spot empty again. Every day gets a little easier. The pain is still profound, but I cry less.

The unmistakable rumble sounds behind me, so I run to the elevator. If I can get inside and push the close button, I won't have to see him. I know seeing him will crush me. As I rush to the elevator, he climbs out of his car.

"Good morning, Katarina." He calls after me. "How's your day going?"

It was going fine until you sucker-punched me in the stomach by showing up this morning.

He slides into the elevator and pushes the button for my floor and his.

A smile wavers on my lips. "Good morning, Mr. Noble. I hope you have a great day."

His eyes widen. "I asked you how your day is going."

Despite the dark circles under his eyes, he's still handsome, and it hurts to look at him.

"It's just beginning, so it would be premature to say."

The elevator stops, and I bolt as fast as I can. Standing near him is more than I can handle. The scent of him takes me to places my memory can't visit.

I run to my desk and burst into tears.

"Katarina, are you okay?"

Trevor walks through my door, closes, and locks it. When he reaches me, he pulls me into his arms.

"Oh ... Trevor," I wail. "I thought I'd be okay, but I'm not. I saw him, and it broke my heart—again. How many times is a man allowed to do that?"

I sob so much I get hiccups.

"It'll be okay. I know you feel you won't survive, but you will. I had a bad breakup several years ago, and I didn't leave my bed for a week. You're here every day, and that proves how strong you are. You didn't fall in love with him overnight, and you won't fall out of love with him that fast either."

"How long did it take before you felt like you could move on?"

"You don't want to know. All you need to do is breathe. You did it before him, and you'll do it after him. How about lunch today?"

"Lunch sounds great." The universe smiled on me the day Trevor became my boss.

After we eat, Trevor declares the afternoon is paid downtime. Who am I to argue? He's my boss.

Trevor believes the best therapy for depression is shopping. We visit several boutiques and a store that creates custom perfume. When we get back to Noble Enterprises, we smell good and look great.

We part ways at the elevator. He goes to his office, and I go home to hang my new clothes and drink another bottle of wine.

As always at this time of day, the traffic is bumper-to-bumper. Looking straight ahead, I'm jolted into shock when I'm hit from behind.

The impact sends my Jetta barreling into the intersection, where a car entering from the opposite direction broadsides me.

Everything takes on an eerie silence in the aftermath. I think I'm okay, but my left arm hurts like a bitch. Bile rises to my throat as sweat runs down my forehead. I reach up to swipe it away, but my hand comes back covered in blood.

"Ma'am, are you okay?" A young man asks, sticking his head through the window. His blue eyes are pretty, but not Viking god pretty. "I called the police and an ambulance. Don't move. I don't want you to hurt yourself more."

Hurt myself more? Sure, my arm hurts, and I feel pain in my face and chest from the impact of the airbags, but I'm okay. I look around to see every window is shattered except for the passenger side.

"Shit. This will cost a fortune to fix."

Within minutes, there are police, firefighters, and paramedics everywhere. Somehow, they pull me from my car and place me on a gurney.

As I'm rolling to the waiting ambulance, I remember my shopping bags in the back seat. There is no way I'm going anywhere without them. That's two weeks' salary in those bags, and I argue with the medical staff to get them. There's a stick from the IV needle, then nothing.

"KAT, open your eyes, sweetie. It's Em."

I hear her voice, but it's far away. My eyes are heavy, and all I want to do is sleep.

I open them and see the fuzzy outline of people—Em, Chris,

Trevor, and my parents. Rose is here, too. Why are so many people in my room?

"Katarina, honey? It's your mother. Wake up so Dr. Noble can check you out. She stayed late to see you."

"What? Where am I?" I wince at the pain. "Holy hell, my arm and head are killing me."

"Katarina, it's Rose. You were in a bad car accident. You broke your arm and needed a few stitches on your forehead, but everything else seems okay. That little car of yours saved your life."

"My car ... is it okay? I need it for work."

"You're staying here overnight for observation. If everything looks good tomorrow morning, you can go home," Rose lays a comforting hand on my shoulder—the only place that doesn't hurt.

"I have work tomorrow." I think about the clothes. "I need my new clothes for work." I ramble on about shopping and my schedule, but it makes little sense.

"Nonsense. You'll stay because I said so. Your clothes are fine. The paramedics brought them in. They said you wouldn't let them transport you until they had them in the ambulance. They had to sedate you to calm you down. You weren't complaining about the pain, you wanted those darn clothes."

"I have no clothes. Mine are at Damon's, and I can't get them because I love him too..." The effect of pain medication takes me to dreamland.

THE SQUEEZING of my arm wakes me with a start. I open my eyes to see the nurse removing a blood pressure cuff. Sitting to my left is Damon. He is holding the fingers that peek out of my cast and lightly caressing them with his thumb, back and forth.

"My mom called me and told me." He looks around the empty room. "Your family went home several hours ago, but they'll check on you tomorrow. Do you need anything? You're allowed to have ice chips. Let me get you some."

Within minutes, he's back and feeding me ice chips. They're so good because I'm so thirsty.

"Are you in pain, Angel? I can ask them to give you pain meds if you need it."

"Why are you here?"

"Katarina, no matter how you feel about me, I care about you. Can we forget what happened last week for today? I want to be here with you. If you want me to leave, you have to kick me out."

"It's not that I don't want you here, but it's hard for me when you're near."

Damon wasn't put together like usual. His hair was mussed, his jacket a wrinkled mess, and his tie was gone.

"Do you want me to leave?"

Did I? Waking up to him beside me was like a dream. "No, I don't. I don't want to be by myself," I confess.

"I'll be here every time you open your eyes," he promises.

True to his word, he spends the night with me in the hospital. It seems like a selfless act, but I can't analyze his motives now.

Em walks in and scowls. "I've got this under control. You can leave," she tells Damon.

"Do you need help getting her home?" he asks.

"Nope. We got it taken care of," she snaps.

There's a look of resignation in his eyes when he leans over and places a chaste kiss on my cheek.

"I'll check in on you later." He walks out of the door and my life again.

"What was he doing here?" Em asks. "I couldn't believe my eyes when I saw him sitting there."

"Rose called him. He was sweet. Don't worry. It won't change anything. He was here as a concerned friend."

I CAN'T PUT my seat belt on by myself, the stitches in my forehead ache, and I'm tired.

Everyone is at our house when we get home. The only people missing are Rose and Damon.

Chris and Trevor tuck me into bed, and Em and Anthony make sure I've eaten. My parents stay to make sure I'm settled before they leave. The doctor said to stay home for the rest of the week.

"Em, tell me the truth about my car. Can it be fixed?" I already know the answer. Rose told me my Jetta sacrificed itself to save me, but I need to hear it.

"There's nothing left of your car. The back end was pushed so far forward, your shopping bags ended up in the front seat. The driver's side is now on the right side of the car. It's totaled."

"How am I supposed to get anywhere?"

She smiles. "We divvied up the driving duties until you get back into a car. You'll probably be able to get behind the wheel in a week, but you have to get off pain meds first."

MY FIRST DAY back feels wonderful. Em drops me off in the employee garage, where the silver Mustang sits in its designated spot with the orange Charger parked next to it.

Trevor meets me on the ground floor and walks with me to my office. Sitting on my desk is a vase of flowers, a set of keys, and a note.

Katarina,

I hope that you're healing well. I checked with my mother, and she said you could safely drive a car. I thought you might like to borrow the Charger until you have time to research and purchase a new one. Please consider my offer.

Yours,
Damon

Offering me the Charger isn't a small thing. It's been in his garage since Roman's death. I don't know what to do about the offer. If I borrow it, it may give him the wrong impression, and if I turn him down, I could hurt his feelings.

Trevor stands nearby like a sentry.

"I'm in a dilemma," I say. "Damon offered to loan me his second car. It's a huge step for him because it has significant meaning to his past. What should I do?"

"I've known Mr. Noble for five years. We haven't become buddies, but he looks after his people. I can't imagine him having any other motive than making sure you're okay. Maybe this is helping him too. He's showing you he can let go of something that means a lot to him."

Trevor's observation takes me by surprise.

"Thank you for your insight. You've given me a lot to think about."

After careful consideration, I text him.

Thank you for the generous offer. I know how difficult it must be to let go of that car. Thanks for the loan. I promise to get it back to you soon.

Kat

I've reverted to my nickname because it's less painful to hear Kat than Katarina.

I'm glad you can use it. I had the tires and the battery changed, so it should be in perfect condition. I'm burying my past, Katarina, so I can move on with my future. The car is a small part of the process. See you Wednesday at six.

Wednesday seemed so far away when I picked that day. I'm shocked at how quickly time passes.

I'm proud of you, Damon, and thanks for the loaner.

The keys feel cold as I run them through my fingers. The ring contains two keys and a key chain. One key is distinctly a car key, the other a house key. The key chain is an angel.

What am I going to do with this man?

CHAPTER THIRTY

It's Wednesday, and I'm in the garage at Ahz. The Mustang is parked down the aisle, and the sight of it makes my heart flutter.

The last time I saw Damon was at the hospital and all I wanted was for him to crawl into bed and hold me. My emotions are tangled when it comes to him.

I'm passionately in love with him, but I can't settle for anything less than all of him. Growing up, I never fantasized about loving a man who could only love me halfway.

My panic rises when I reach the door. I bend over, trying to put my head between my knees so that I don't faint.

"Are you okay?" His voice startles me as he rushes forward.

"Yes. Fine. Feeling a little lightheaded. I guess I still get nervous driving after the accident," I lie. The only thing I'm nervous about is this meeting with him.

We walk together into the restaurant. The maître d takes us to a private table.

"You look awful. You need more sleep, and you need to eat better."

"Thank you. Saying I look awful starts dinner off perfectly." Sarcasm oozes from me.

"I'm sorry. It's been several days since I saw you, and you've lost weight. You don't look rested. Despite that, you're still beautiful."

"I don't need to worry about my diet because Greta feeds me daily. That is no doubt, a directive from you."

"If she's bringing you lunch, she's doing it on her own. I have no control over my staff any longer. They circled the wagons around you. They won't answer questions or tell me anything. I've tried to check on you. I ask Trevor, and he hangs up on me. Greta won't even talk to me. The only information I get is from Emma—if she answers, and it's always a curt 'she's fine.'"

I laugh.

"It's not funny. I'm the damn president of my company, and none of my employees return my calls."

"I'm sorry. You're right, it's not funny, but believe me when I say I've got nothing to do with it."

"They like you more than they like me, and I get it because I like you better than I like me, too."

Over dinner, we sip wine and prepare ourselves for a difficult conversation. Once the coffee comes, he begins.

"Katarina, first and foremost, I need you to know I didn't invite her to the grand opening. She came with a guy named Tory Blake, and although you saw a kiss, I didn't kiss her."

"I understand all that," I tell him.

"Then why aren't we together? Why are you not lying in my arms every night? Why do I feel like my life ended on Friday night?"

Tears prick at my eyes.

"We can't be together because I'll never be okay with happy and content. I want love. I want someone to love me like his life depends on it."

"But I do."

"You only feel that way because not loving me means losing me.

The one thing I know about you is you'll get what you want no matter the cost, and my heart is too priceless to use as a pawn."

"I don't want to hurt you." He reaches across the table to touch my fingers.

Just that little touch does things to me. It makes me want to forget everything that's happened and crawl into his lap, but I can't.

"You have to love yourself before you can love me. You have to let go of your past to have a future. You'll never be able to love me until you let go of Mara."

"I'm not interested in Mara." He sits back and runs his hand through his hair. It falls messily across his forehead the way it does after we make love.

"You're not over her. I don't know what she did to you, but whatever it was, it put your life on hold for a decade. Will you need another to figure it out? I don't have ten years to wait. I want to fall in love, get married, and have children. I want things you can't give me."

"She slept with my brother!" he screams in anguish.

What can I say to that? I'm sorry doesn't scratch the surface.

A single tear runs down his cheek. He swipes it from his face, rises from his seat, and leaves, but I can't move.

It didn't happen to me, but I can imagine the pain and betrayal he feels. The two people he loved above everything else deceived him, and then one of them died before he could get closure.

CHAPTER THIRTY-ONE

Damon disappears without a word. I text and call, but he doesn't answer.

Days later, Rose calls.

"Katarina, where is my son? I haven't heard from him. His housekeeper says he hasn't been home since Wednesday morning."

My heart falls to the pit of my stomach. "I don't know, Rose. Damon and I aren't together. We had dinner Wednesday, and he left abruptly. I haven't seen him since."

"I know you had a little disagreement, but I didn't think it was something that would break you up. What happened?"

I only give her the information about what happened at Ahz. If Damon wants his mom to know the rest, he needs to tell her himself.

"I'll help you find him."

"Thank you." She already sounds like the worry aged her. "I've lost one son, and I can't lose another."

I'm frozen with fear because I know what Damon looked like when he left the restaurant. He was a broken man.

I grab my purse and keys and run for the door.

My first stop is his house. I key in the code to the gate and thank God he put his house key on the ring.

I move through the house, calling his name, but he's not there.

My clothes are strewn across his bed, making it clear he slept with them. It breaks my heart to know how much he's hurting.

My next stop is Noble Enterprises. As soon as I enter the garage, I know he isn't here because the Mustang is missing.

Entering Ahz, I scour the garage, but he's not there either. I check the local hospitals and call the police to make sure he hasn't been detained. No one has heard from him or seen him.

I drive to Griffith Park Observatory because he said he goes there to think, but I don't find him.

I sit in the driver's seat and think about where he'd go to feel connected or safe? It hits me, and I can't drive fast enough.

I make it to Brentwood in record time and find his childhood home. His car is nowhere in sight, but somehow, I know he's here. I can feel him.

I park the Charger and run to the backyard. If he isn't here, I don't know what I will do. The rope ladder swings in the breeze. With trepidation, I take one rung at a time.

At the top, I peek over the edge and see him curled up on his side. He hasn't shaved in days. He's in the same suit he wore when I saw him at Ahz, but despite being in disarray, he's still an exquisite man.

"Damon, I'm here. I'm here, baby." I lie down and spoon him. "Turn over and let me look at you."

"Oh, Katarina, are you here?"

"I'm here."

He turns and stares at me.

"I can't do this without you. My life is nothing unless you're in it."

I sit up and guide his head into my lap while I run my fingers through his hair. I cradle him for over an hour.

How can I not love this man?

Looking up toward the sky to pray, I see another set of initials carved into the ceiling. The letters are mine and encased in a heart.

"Let's go home, honey. We can clean you up, and I'll make dinner. If you want, we'll snuggle on the couch."

I get him down the ladder and into the Charger.

The closer we get to his house, the more alive he becomes. As soon as we are inside, I take him upstairs, start the shower, and text his mother to tell her he's safe.

With the jets set, I turn my attention to caring for him.

"Katarina, you don't have to do this. I can get myself in the shower. I'm okay now." He shrugs out of his jacket and takes off his shirt. He's thinner—almost frail looking. "Thank you for coming. It's good to know you still care."

"I'm here because I love you, and I want to take care of you. Now, let's get you in the shower."

Finding a plastic bag under the sink, I wrap my cast and climb in behind him. For the next fifteen minutes, I make sure Damon is clean from head to toe.

Once out of the shower, I dry him and dress him in sweatpants and a T-shirt and tuck into his bed.

"I'll be right back. I'm just getting you dinner."

With a glass of water in one hand and a bowl of spaghetti in the other, I return to him.

He's curled in on himself and looks as small and timid as a child. He faces me when I enter.

"You don't have to stay." I know he says that for my benefit, but I can tell that he'd prefer I stay.

"I remember a man sitting beside my hospital bed. He remained with me even though no one wanted him there but me. If you don't want me here, then I'll leave, but I want to stay."

"I can't have you stay if you plan to leave me again. I won't survive that." His head falls back to the bed.

I can't leave him because I love him. He has so much shit to wade through, but I don't expect him to do it alone.

"A while ago, we said we'd take it one kiss at a time, and I'm still willing to do that." I sit on the bed beside him. "I'm sorry I left you when you needed me the most. I may never forgive myself for that."

He pulls himself up and leans against the headboard.

"You were right to leave me. I was holding on to the past, but you're wrong about one thing. I don't love Mara. I love the memory of Mara because when she was around, so was Roman." He reaches up and touches a strand of my hair. "When she kissed me, I felt nothing. They weren't your lips. She had the wrong feel and taste and smell. I tried to hold on to the memory of the brother I loved, not the one who hurt me. Not the one who betrayed me."

"What they did is unforgivable. Do you think his condition made it difficult for him to think straight? Maybe he wasn't in his right mind." I swirl a bite of pasta on the fork and feed him.

"I thought about that, but I can't give him an easy out, and Mara has no excuse at all. Roman was an asshole, and she was a selfish bitch."

He takes another bite. We continue that way, a bite and talk until the bowl is empty. With his belly full, he settles back and sighs.

"When he died that June, I tried to adopt my mother's perception of him. What I knew in my head never matched the truth in my heart, and it messed me up. I can't get the vision of walking in on them out of my head. When he saw me, his response was classic Roman. He looked at me and told me to go screw myself, because after having him, Mara wouldn't have anyone else."

"That's awful."

"I got my nose broken for losing a baseball mitt, and he got nothing for stealing my life. Days later, he found out about the leukemia. I never talked to him again. He died June fifteenth with no one there but our mother. I still hate him. Not because he stole my past but because he's stealing my future." He sets his hand on my shoulder. "You're my future, and I won't let him or Mara take you from me."

His body folds around mine. He fits me like we were custom made for each other.

"It'll be okay," I whisper.

We slide down on the bed. He curls around me, and I'm happy to be in his arms.

"Don't give up on me," he whispers.

"I won't."

I SWEAR HE KISSED ME. I know he kissed me, but his words made little sense. "I'll be back."

I fell back to sleep and dreamed of Terminator.

I walk downstairs, expecting to find him. Instead, there's a note on the counter.

Katarina,

Thank you for being there and giving me love I don't deserve. I have a few things to take care of before I can offer you more but don't doubt that I will. With you, I want everything. The house, the kids, the gray hair. Give me a little time. I'm coming back, and I hope you'll be waiting for me.

This isn't me running from you. It's me clearing the path so I can run to you.

I spoke to my mother, and she knows everything. I didn't want to put you in a position where you thought you needed to protect me. She respects you, and I never want to jeopardize the friendship you have with her.

Please take this time to think about what you want. I want it all, but I'll take whatever you'll offer. It wasn't until you walked away that I realized how much I love you and how much I lost.

Yours Forever,

Damon

PS – I changed the code on the gate to 0 3 1 0. It's the day my life began. It's the day I met you.

His letter leaves me speechless. He loves me, and I believe him.

AS THE DAYS PASS, I fall into a routine. Each morning, there are flowers and a handwritten note from Damon. Every one of them ends with "I love you."

I glimpsed him climbing into the elevator once. He blew me a kiss before the door closed.

By the time I made it to his office, he was gone, but Greta handed me a note.

I love you. Wait for me.

Yours Forever,

Damon

Monday night, I dine with Chris and Trevor, who are moving in the right direction. Tuesday, Rose and I eat at the Greek restaurant and talk in-depth about the situation between Damon and Roman.

Emma spends most of her time with Anthony, but they always invite me to whatever they're doing. I always decline because watching them makes me miss Damon more.

Rose is having a party for a colleague who is retiring and has enlisted my help.

She says I met him at the Philharmonic, but I don't remember. Damon was right, she introduced me to everyone but the orchestra.

The extravagant affair is at her Brentwood estate this weekend, and I'm grateful she keeps me busy because left on my own, my mind wanders to Damon and what he's up to.

As if I summoned him. His name pops up on my phone. "Damon," I say breathlessly. "Where are you?"

"I'm close, Angel. Open the door."

I drop my phone and run to the front door. When I swing it open, he's standing there, wearing jeans, a snug T-shirt and a smile.

I fling myself into his arms and press my lips to his while he grabs my bottom and lifts me.

"What a greeting. Can we do that again?" His eyes are clear, and his complexion is healthy. He looks damn good.

"You want to go outside and have me open the door again? Can't we continue the kisses?"

"Definitely kisses, and then we need to talk."

My heart drops to my stomach. Is this where he tells me he doesn't love me? That thought goes out the window when he kisses me again. A man who doesn't love me or need me wouldn't kiss me like his life depended on it.

When we're breathless, he carries me to the couch and sets me down.

"God, I've missed you."

I scoot as close to him as I can without crawling onto his lap. "Where have you been?"

He smiles. "I told you. I'm clearing a path. I sold my childhood house. I spent time at Roman's grave. I even talked to Mara."

I stiffen when he mentions her name. "Mara got to see you, and I didn't?"

He tugs me onto his lap. "No, Angel. We talked on the phone."

"Why did she do it?"

"She doesn't know, and I'm not going to guess. I think she's sorry. One thing I told her was we can't ever go back. We need to move forward. She's in the past and has no place in my future." He caresses my cheek with his knuckles and looks deep into my eyes. "I love you."

"I love you too, but why couldn't I help you?"

"This was something I needed to do alone. That's why I told you I'd be back and asked you to wait. I love you, Katarina. I think I loved you that first night, but I didn't recognize the truth."

"Will you stay with me tonight?"

He leans in until we touch foreheads. "That sounds amazing, but I can't. Mom's having her shindig tomorrow, and she needs my help."

Disappointment weighs me down.

"You'll be there tomorrow?"

"Tomorrow and always." He moves me from his lap and stands. "I'll see you then." He presses the sweetest kiss to my lips before he leaves. Only this time, I know I'll see him again.

CHAPTER THIRTY-TWO

I arrive early at Rose's place. I still can't get over the beauty of the gardens. The caterers set up tables throughout the space so guests can enjoy both the indoor and outdoor areas. People will arrive at six o'clock.

"You're here." Rose rushes over and kisses my cheek. She stands back and looks at my green maxi dress. "You look lovely." She takes my arm and guides me to a room down a hallway.

"Feel free to wear what you're wearing, but I shopped yesterday and found this beautiful ice-blue cocktail dress on sale at Nordie's. You absolutely do not have to wear it, but it reminds me of the dress Damon bought you for the Philharmonic."

"Is he here?"

"Not yet. He called and said he's running late, but he'll be here."

The disappointment pulls my shoulders forward. I miss him because I miss our life together. I miss sex, his smile, and his bossiness. I miss everything about him.

Rose lifts my chin. "Don't worry, he's coming." She nods toward the dress hanging from a knob on the nearby dresser. "Wear the dress, or don't wear it. It's up to you." She kisses my cheek. "Everything will be wonderful." She leaves me alone with a dress the exact color of Damon's eyes.

I slip into it and find that it fits perfectly. Something tells me Rose didn't buy this dress either. The fit is too perfect, and the style is more Damon than his mother.

People trickle in, and by six thirty, the party is in full swing. It's not a dinner, but drinks and appetizers. I graze the tables and wait like everyone else for the guest of honor to arrive. I'm more antsy because Damon is still MIA. My eyes are constantly on the door, watching for him.

Rose stands on the second step of the grand staircase and taps her wineglass with a spoon. I turn to scan the crowd, still looking for Damon but glimpse someone who looks like Em. I take a step in that direction but realize there's another stunning redhead at the party.

"Where are you headed, young lady? I need you here with me." Rose waves me over and points to a spot in front of the stairs. "Stand right there."

"Ladies and gentlemen, thanks for coming today," Rose walks up the stairs to stand a level above. "This is a special time in my life. As you know, I lost a husband and a son to cancer, and I nearly lost Damon to oversight and ignorance. A wonderful woman named Katarina Cross met my son and changed his life forever. She gave him love, encouragement, and hope for a bright future. She's here tonight under the guise of throwing a retirement party for a colleague." She spreads her arms to the crowd. "All of you are here because you either know my son or you know Katarina. Damon is here tonight because he's helplessly in love."

A thousand butterflies swarm my insides. Damon steps out a nearby room and joins his mother at the top of the stairs. He's dressed in a black tuxedo that fits him to perfection. He smiles, but it's not just his lips, it's his eyes that smile too; eyes full of love, hope, and passion.

"Good evening, everyone." He waves to the crowd and kisses his mom on the cheek. She turns and descends the stairs. "Hello, Angel," he stares at me, and I swear we're the only two people in the room. "Several months ago, I met this amazing woman. Hold up your hand, Katarina, so everyone can see you."

I raise my hand a little, but I'm embarrassed by the attention. Several people crowd around me, and when I look, my parents and Greta are on one side, and Chris, Trevor, and Rose are on the other. Anthony and Emma are standing next to the stairs. The people I love surround me.

"We met unconventionally—a blind date of sorts, but I knew the day I met her, I'd never let her go. She's a little thing, but she packs an incredible amount of strength in her five-foot-four frame. She has to be strong to put up with me. So many people show you what they think you want to see, but Katarina shows you who she is." He looks at my parents. "I'm so grateful for her parents, who raised her with love and gave her the freedom to be herself."

Looking back at the crowd, Damon says, "She got to see the real me, and it wasn't pretty, but she loved me despite it all, and she didn't give up on me." He takes a deep breath. "I'm a damaged person. So much sorrow has touched my life, and I never imagined I'd feel happy again. She changed everything. If you'll humor me for a moment, I'd like to take the time to tell her what's in my heart."

Tears fill my eyes. Not only does this man care for me, but he's publicly declaring it.

Rose walks over and leans in to whisper, "Give my boy a chance, Katarina. He won't disappoint you."

"The first time I met Katarina, I asked her about her prerequisites for dating, and she informed me that I had to have nice teeth and not be a serial killer."

Everyone laughs.

Damon walks down a few steps and hands Emma two envelopes. She brings them to me and places them into my palm.

"Katarina, there are two envelopes in your hand. One is a letter from my dentist confirming I'm cavity-free and up to date on my cleanings. He even went as far as to say I have excellent teeth." The crowd laughs again. "The second is a full background check. No run-ins with the law, and my credit rating is stellar. I'm offering you full disclosure. There is nothing I'll hide from you. Most importantly, I want to tell the world I love you. I've lived too long without you and refuse to spend another minute alone. You are my heart and my soul, and without you, I'm less."

He walks down the steps until he's in front of me with his eyes looking into mine.

"Damon, I love you. I always have." I place my palm over his rapidly beating heart. "I want all of you. Including the heart you claimed to not have."

He places his hands on my waist and pulls me closer. "I'm yours for as long as you'll have me, and I hope it's forever. My heart belongs to you." He leans forward and brushes his lips across mine. "I'd love to start over again. Can I take you to dinner?"

"Dinner, Damon?" I make a tsk tsk sound. "There's no moving backward."

He speaks to the crowd. "She's a risk-taker and is willing to take me on. If you don't mind, I'd like to start forever right now. Enjoy the food and drinks."

He lifts me into his arms and turns me around in circles. When his lips press against mine, I'm whole again.

The crowd's hoots and hollers fade as we near the front door.

I don't know where we're headed, but when he whispers, "Relax and enjoy," I know I'm going somewhere I've never been.

Do you want a Bonus Scene? Click here to see Damon and Katarina in this Epilogue.

NEXT UP IS *Yours to Conquer*

GET A FREE BOOK.

Go to www.authorkellycollins.com

OTHER BOOKS BY KELLY COLLINS

A Pure Decadence Series

Yours to Have

Yours to Conquer

Yours to Protect

A Pure Decadence Collection

Recipes for Love

A Tablespoon of Temptation

A Pinch of Passion

A Dash of Desire

A Cup of Compassion

A Dollop of Delight

A Layer of Love

Recipe for Love Collection 1-3

Recipe for Love Collection 4-6

ABOUT THE AUTHOR

International bestselling author of more than thirty novels, Kelly Collins writes with the intention of keeping love alive. Always a romantic, she blends real-life events with her vivid imagination to create characters and stories that lovers of contemporary romance, new adult, and romantic suspense will return to again and again.

For More Information
www.authorkellycollins.com
kelly@authorkellycollins.com

Printed in Great Britain
by Amazon